A Merger…
Or Marriage?

RAEANNE THAYNE

◎™ MILLS & BOON®

Pure reading pleasure™

First published in Great Britain 2009
by Harlequin Mills & Boon Limited,
Eton House, 18-24 Paradise Road, Richmond, Surrey TW9 1SR

© Harlequin Books S.A. 2008

ISBN: 978 0 263 87046 6

23-0609

Harlequin Mills & Boon policy is to use papers that are
natural, renewable and recyclable products and made from
wood grown in sustainable forests. The logging and
manufacturing processes conform to the legal environmental
regulations of the country of origin.

Printed and bound in Spain
by Litografia Rosés S.A., Barcelona

Friends? Is that what she called it?

Richard heard Anna's explanation of their relationship with a mixture of anger and disbelief.

What the hell was she doing here? Why hadn't someone warned him?

He had heard that Anna was working for Northeastern HealthCare, he just had never dreamed she would be on board for the conglomerate's hostile takeover attempts at Walnut River General.

How could she sit across the boardroom table, all cool and gorgeous like some kind of damn Viking princess, acting as if her very presence wasn't a betrayal of everything her family had done for this hospital and this town?

Yeah, he had been crazy about Anna once. But it had been a long, long time ago.

RAEANNE THAYNE

finds inspiration in the beautiful northern Utah mountains, where she lives with her husband and three children. Her books have won numerous honours, including a RITA® nomination from Romance Writers of America and a Career Achievement Award from *Romantic Times BOOKreviews* magazine. RaeAnne loves to hear from readers and can be reached through her website at www.raeannethayne.com.

Chapter One

So this was what it felt like to be a pariah.

Anna Wilder tilted her chin slightly higher, tightened her grasp on her briefcase and walked firmly past the two gray-haired biddies at the information desk in the lobby of Walnut River General Hospital.

She didn't need to keep them in view to feel the heat of their glares following her to the gleaming elevator doors. She also didn't need to fully hear their whispers to catch enough to make her ulcer go into overdrive.

It's her, Anna Wilder.

The traitor.

James and Alice must be rolling in their graves.

She did her best to ignore them—and the hurt that settled like greasy black bile in her stomach. Still, to her great shame, she wasn't quite able to control the slight tremble of her hand as she pushed the elevator button to go up.

One of the two cars appeared to be permanently stuck on the second floor but the other one at last began creeping downward in what felt like excruciatingly painful slow motion.

She prayed the blasted thing would hurry up and arrive— not only to allow her to slip inside and escape the stares and whispers but, more importantly, because she was late.

She really hated being late.

The elevator stopped on the second floor and paused there for a few moments before continuing its descent. Suddenly a new apprehension fluttered her ulcer.

Why hadn't she been smart enough to take the stairs? The only thing worse than being late for her meeting would be the social discomfort of encountering one of her siblings in the elevator during her first few minutes at the hospital.

She didn't know which one would be harder to face right now. Ella? Peter? David? It probably didn't matter. They were all furious with her and would no doubt love a chance to let her know.

Just before the elevator arrived, one of the two volunteers at the information desk raised her voice in what had to be deliberate malice so Anna couldn't miss her words.

"She might have the Wilder name," she said in a carrying voice, "but she's not a true Wilder. How can she be, since she's in bed with those who are trying to sell out this hospital and this town?"

Anna inhaled sharply. Apparently the doctors weren't the only ones at Walnut River General who could wield a scalpel. The words effectively sliced straight to where she was most vulnerable.

Her hand tightened on the briefcase as she ruthlessly tried to ignore the hot tears burning behind her eyelids.

It didn't matter what a couple of dried-up old prunes had to say about her. Why should it? They had nothing better to do with their time than sit around gossiping and watching all the human suffering march through their lobby.

She knew she was doing the right thing—the *best* thing—for Walnut River and its citizens. She just had to convince everybody else in town.

No problem.

At long, long last, the elevator car arrived and the doors whooshed open. She considered it nothing short of a miracle that it was blessedly empty. Not a Wilder in sight.

Only after the doors slid shut did she close her eyes and slump against the wall of the elevator, pressing a hand to her stomach before she dug in the pocket of her suit jacket for an antacid.

She did not want to be here. In Walnut River, at the hospital her family had all but founded, in this blasted elevator.

It helped nothing that she had expected the reaction she had received from those two volunteers and she expected much more vitriol in the days ahead.

She had read the reports and knew the merger she had been sent here to expedite wasn't popular among the staff at WRG. Not that she had needed reports. Her family's unreasonable opposition was all the evidence she needed. They had all made no secret that they were furious at her.

Traitor.

Not a Wilder.

She screwed her eyes shut. Focus on the job, she chanted to herself. That was all that mattered. Move in fast and hard and wrap things up so she could return to New York.

She had no choice, not if she wanted to keep her job. And she certainly did.

She loved working for Northeastern HealthCare, one of the fastest growing health care conglomerates in the region. She was on the fast track there and had great hopes of making vice president within the next five years. That goal would be even closer if she could pull this deal off.

Mercifully, though the elevator stopped on the second floor to pick up a couple of nurses, she didn't recognize them and they didn't seem to know her. One of them even gave her a friendly smile.

So maybe David hadn't yet gotten around to plastering up wanted posters throughout the hospital of her wearing devil horns.

Beware of the evil HMO-mongerer.

She wouldn't put anything past her second-oldest brother, a gifted plastic surgeon who had recently returned to Walnut River as well. Unlike her, he had come back to a warm welcome, embraced by one and all—the prodigal son giving up a lucrative career in L.A. as plastic surgeon to the stars to share his brilliance with patients in his own hometown.

On the fourth floor, the nurses exited with her. Anna stood for a moment, trying to catch her bearings.

This part of the hospital had been renovated in the past few years and she was slightly disoriented at the changes.

She remembered it as slightly old-fashioned, with wood-grained paneling and dark carpeting. Now everything was light and airy, with new windows and a far more modern feel.

"Do you need help finding something?" one of the nurses asked, noticing her confusion.

"Yes. Thanks. I'm looking for the administrator's office."

"Down the hall. Second door on the right," she said.

"Thank you." Anna gave a polite smile, grateful for any help she could find here in this hostile environment, then headed in the direction the woman indicated.

The receptionist's nameplate read Tina Tremaine. She greeted Anna with a friendly smile, her features warm and open.

"Hello. I'm Anna Wilder. I'm here for a three-o'clock meeting with the hospital attorney and the administrator."

The instant she heard Anna's name, the woman's smile slid away as if a cold breeze had just blown through the room.

"I'm here for a three o'clock meeting with the hospital attorney and the administrator."

"Phil Crandall, the hospital attorney, is not here yet, Ms. Wilder. But Mr. Sumner and your attorney are in the boardroom. They're waiting for you."

Though she spoke politely enough, Anna thought she saw a tiny sliver of disdain in the woman's eyes.

She fished around in her mind for something she might say to alter the woman's negative impression, then checked the impulse.

She was working hard to break the habits of a lifetime, that hunger for approval she couldn't quite shake. Did it really matter what J.D.'s receptionist thought of her? It certainly wouldn't change anything about her mission here in Walnut River.

"Thank you," she answered, mustering a smile she hoped was at least polite if not completely genuine. She headed for the door the receptionist indicated, tilting her chin up and hoping she projected confidence and competence.

This was it. Her chance to cinch the promotion at NHC and cement her growing reputation as a rainmaker there.

Or she could blow the merger, lose her job, and end up begging on the street somewhere.

Think positive, she ordered herself. *You can do this. You've done it before.* As she pushed open the door, she visualized herself handing over the signed deal to her bosses, both her direct supervisor, Wallace Jeffers—vice president for mergers and acquisitions—and the NHC chief executive officer who had given her this assignment, Alfred Daly.

It was a heady, enticing image, one she clung to as she faced the two men at the boardroom table, papers spread out in front of them.

Two men sat at a boardroom table talking, papers spread out in front of them. She knew both of them and smiled at J. D. Sumner and Walter Posey, the NHC attorney.

"I'm sorry if I've kept you waiting. I didn't realize there would be so much construction surrounding the hospital."

J.D. nodded. "Walnut River is growing. You just have to walk outside to see it."

"Which is one factor that makes this hospital an attractive opportunity for NHC, as you well know."

J.D. had first come to Walnut River as an employee of NHC. He had ended up falling—literally—for her sister, Ella, resigning from NHC and taking the job as hospital administrator.

She didn't know all the details but she knew Ella had treated J.D. after he was injured in a bad tumble on some icy steps when leaving the hospital. Something significant must have happened between them to compel a man like

J.D. to fall for his orthopedic surgeon and leave a promising career at Northeastern HealthCare to take the reins of Walnut River General Hospital.

She couldn't imagine giving up everything she had worked so hard to attain for something as ephemeral as love, but she had to admit part of her envied her sister. J.D. must love Ella very much.

She could only hope his relationship with Ella had turned him soft. Judging by his track record at NHC, Anna feared he would be a formidable foe in her efforts to make the merger happen.

"Our attorney was caught up in the traffic snarl, as well," J.D. answered. "He just called and was still parking his car but he should be here any moment."

Though he spoke cordially enough, there was a reserve in his voice she couldn't miss.

She had only known him casually when he worked for NHC, but their interactions as coworkers had always been marked by friendly respect. Now, though, they were on opposite sides of what was shaping up to be an ugly fight over the future of the hospital.

He didn't seem antagonistic, as she had feared, only distant. She had to admit she was relieved. He and Ella were engaged, from what she understood. This was bound to be awkward enough between them without outright antipathy.

"I'm going for some coffee before we get started," the NHC attorney announced. "Can I get either of you anything?"

Anna shook her head at Walter, whom she had worked with before on these due diligence reviews. "None for me, thanks."

"Sumner?"

J.D. shook his head. "I'm good."

As soon as Walter left the room, J.D. leaned back in his chair and studied her carefully, until Anna squirmed under the weight of his green-eyed gaze.

"So how are you? I mean, how are you *really?*"

She blinked at the unexpected personal question and was slow to answer, choosing her words carefully. "I'm managing. I suppose you heard I tried to stay out of this one, obviously without success."

He nodded, his brow furrowed. "I heard. Does Daly really think your family connection will make anyone happier about NHC's efforts to take over the hospital?"

"Hope springs eternal, I suppose," she muttered.

J.D. laughed. "Alfred Daly obviously doesn't know your stubborn siblings, does he?"

If her boss had any idea what he was up against, Anna had a feeling he never would have initiated the merger proceedings at Walnut River General.

"How's Ella?" The question slipped out before she could yank it back.

J.D.'s eyes widened with surprise for just an instant that she would ask before they softened into a dreamy kind of look that filled her with no small amount of envy.

"She's great. Wonderful. Except the wedding next month is making her a little crazy. I told her to just leave the details to someone else, but she won't hear of it." He paused. "She misses you."

I miss her, too. The words tangled on her tongue and dried there. She couldn't say them, of course. She could never tell J.D. how she hated this distance between her and her sister.

They used to be so close—best friends as well as sisters, only a year apart. They had shared everything—clothes, secrets, friends.

She remembered lying on her stomach in their back-yard, daydreaming and giggling over boys.

"You're going to be my maid of honor," Ella declared more than once. "And I'll be yours."

"One of us will have to get married first," she remembered answering. "So one of us will have to be a matron of honor."

"That sounds so old! Like one of the gray-haired ladies at the hospital! How about we'll both still be maids of honor, even if one of us is already married?"

Anna remembered shaking her head at Ella's twisted logic but in the end, she had agreed, just like she usually did.

That had always been their plan. But now Ella and J.D. were getting married in a month and Anna wasn't even sure she would receive an invitation.

Especially not if she successfully carried out her objective of making this merger a reality.

Her career or her family.

A miserable choice.

"You should talk to her," J.D. said into the silence, with a sudden gentleness that made her want to cry again.

"I wish this were something that a little conversation could fix," she murmured. "I'm afraid it's not that easy."

"You never know until you try," he answered.

She didn't know how to answer him, and to her relief she was spared from having to try when the door opened.

She looked up, expecting Walter with his coffee, then she felt her jaw sag as recognition filtered through.

"Sorry I'm late, J.D. That traffic is a nightmare," the

newcomer said. He was tall and lean, with hair like sunlight shooting through gold flakes. His features were classically handsome—long lashes, a strong blade of a nose, a mouth that was firm and decisive.

The eight years since she had seen Richard Green had definitely been kind to him. He had always been sexy, the sort of male women always looked twice at. When they were teenagers, he couldn't seem to go anywhere without a horde of giggling girls around him, though he had barely seemed to notice them.

Now there was an edge of danger about him, a lean, lithe strength she found compelling and seductive.

J.D. rose and shook his hand. "I appreciate you filling in for Phil at the last minute."

"No problem."

The attorney looked over J.D.'s shoulder and she saw shock and disbelief flicker across the stunning blue eyes that had lost none of their punch even after eight years.

"Anna!"

In a different situation, she might have rushed to hug him but he was sending out a definite "back off" vibe.

"You two know each other, obviously," J.D. said.

She managed to wrench her gaze away from Richard, wondering how she could possibly have forgotten his sheer masculine beauty—and how she ever could have walked away from it in the first place.

The reminder of how things had ended between them sent a flicker of apprehension through her body. He looked less than thrilled to see her. Could this merger become any more complicated? Her family was fighting against her tooth and nail, the hospital administrator was marrying her sister in a month's time, and she and the hospital attorney had a long and tangled history between them.

How was she supposed to be focused and businesslike around Richard when she couldn't help remembering exactly how that mouth had tasted?

"Richard lived only a few blocks away from the house where we were raised," she finally answered J.D., and was appalled to hear the husky note in her voice. She cleared her throat before continuing. "We went to school together and were…good friends."

Friends? Is that what she called it?

Richard listened to her with a mixture of anger and disbelief.

He supposed it wasn't strictly a lie. They had been friends through school. Both had been on similar academic tracks and had belonged to many of the same clubs and after-school organizations. Honor Club, Debate, Key Club. Even later when they went off to different universities, they had stayed in touch and had gotten together as often as possible with their other friends.

Yeah, they had been friends. But there had been much more to it, as she damn well knew, unless she'd somehow managed to conveniently wipe from her memory something that had certainly seemed significant—earthshaking, even—at the time.

What the hell was she doing here? Why hadn't somebody—J.D. or Peter Wilder or Phil Crandall, his absent partner—warned him?

He had heard from Peter and Ella that Anna was working for Northeastern HealthCare, their dreaded enemy. He just had never dreamed she would be a part of the conglomerate's efforts to take over Walnut River General.

She had changed. She used to wear her hair down, a long, luscious waterfall. Now it was tightly contained, pinned back in a sleek style that made her look cool and businesslike. Her features were just as beautiful, though some of the bright, hopeful innocence he remembered in the clear blue of her eyes had faded.

How could she sit across the board-room table, all cool and gorgeous like some kind of damn Viking princess, acting as if her very presence here wasn't a betrayal of everything her family had done for this hospital and for this community?

The depth of his bitterness both shocked and disconcerted him. What did it matter if the NHC executive was Anna Wilder or some other mindless drone they sent?

Either way, the outcome would be the same.

NHC was determined to purchase the hospital from a city council eager to unload it and a solid core of doctors and administrators was just as determined to prevent the deal.

Richard numbered himself among them, even though he was here only in a fill-in capacity for his partner.

Yeah, he had been crazy about Anna once, but it had been a long, long time ago.

That fledgling relationship wasn't significant in the slightest. It hadn't been important enough to her to keep her in Walnut River and whatever might have been between them certainly had no bearing on the current takeover situation.

"Shall we get started with the hearing?" he said icily.

She blinked at his tone—and so did J.D., he noted with some discomfort.

Richard had built a reputation as a cool-headed attorney who never let his personal feelings interfere with his legal responsibilities. He supposed there was a first time for everything.

After a long awkward moment, Anna nodded.

"By all means," she replied, her voice matching his temperature for temperature.

Chapter Two

Two hours later, Richard understood exactly why Anna Wilder had been brought into this takeover.

She was as cold as a blasted icicle and just as hard.

While the NHC attorney had been present to vet the information offered by the hospital side, all of them recognized that Anna was truly the one in charge.

She had been the one leading the discussion, asking the probing questions, never giving an inch as she dissected their answers.

Richard had certainly held his own. Anna might be a tough and worthy opponent but he had one distinct advantage—he was absolutely determined to keep NHC from succeeding in its takeover efforts while he was still alive and kicking.

"Thank you, everyone." Anna stood and surveyed the men around the boardroom table with the sheer aplomb of a boxer standing over the battered and bloody body of an opponent.

"We've covered a great deal of ground. I appreciate your forthrightness and the hospital's compliance with the municipal council's disclosure order. You've been very helpful. I'll take this information back to my superiors and we can go from there."

Richard gritted his teeth. Until they could find a way out of it, the hospital administration had no choice but to comply with the municipal council's strictures.

For now, city council members controlled the purse strings and they appeared eager to escape the costly hospital business that had been a drain on taxpayers for years.

Even the NHC contretemps a few weeks ago involving charges of corporate espionage hadn't dissuaded them.

The only bright spot in the entire takeover attempt was that the municipal council seemed genuinely committed to listening to the opinion of the hospital board of directors before making a final decision to move forward with the sale of the hospital to NHC.

Right now, the board members were leaning only slightly against the sale, though he knew the slightest factor could tip that ultimate decision in either direction.

Who knows? Maybe the NHC bigwigs would take a look at the hospital's tangled financial and personnel disclosures and decide another facility might be more lucrative.

Though he was committed to doing all he could to block the sale, Richard was nothing if not realistic. He wasn't even the hospital's lead attorney, he was only filling in for his partner, who had called begging the favor only an hour before the meeting.

Before he knew Anna Wilder was on board as the NHC

deal-closer, he would have jumped at the chance to step up and handle the merger discussions. Seeing her at the board table with her sleek blond hair yanked ruthlessly into a bun and her brisk business suit and her painfully familiar blue eyes changed everything.

He sighed as he gathered his laptop and papers and slipped them into his briefcase. He was zipping it closed when Anna managed to surprise him yet again, as she had been doing with depressing regularity since he walked into the boardroom.

"Richard, may I speak with you for a moment?"

He checked his watch, his mind on the very important person waiting for him. "I'm afraid I'm in a hurry," he answered.

"Please. This won't take long."

After a moment, he nodded tersely, doing his best to ignore the curious glances from J.D. and the NHC attorney as they both left the room.

Anna closed the door behind the two men and he was suddenly aware of the elegant shape of her fingers against the wood grain and the soft tendrils of hair escaping her pins to curl at the base of her neck.

She had changed perfumes, he noted. In college she had worn something light and flowery that had always reminded him of a sunwarmed garden. Now her scent was slightly more bold—and a hell of a lot more sexy, he had to admit. It curled through the room, tugging at his insides with subtle insistency.

She turned to face him and for an instant, he was blinded by the sheer vibrancy of her smile. "Richard, I know I didn't say this before, but it's really wonderful to see you again! I've wondered so many times how you were."

He found that hard to believe. She had to know where he was. If she had wondered so much, she could have found out as easily as sending a simple e-mail or making a phone call.

"I've been fine. Busy."

Too busy to spend time mooning over the only woman who had ever rejected him, he wanted to add, but managed to refrain.

He was an adult, after all, something he would do well to remember right about now.

"Rumor has it you got married," she said after a moment. "Any kids? I always thought you would make a wonderful father."

"Did you?"

She either missed the bite in his tone or she chose to ignore it.

"I did," she answered. "You were always so great with the neighborhood children. I can remember more than a few impromptu baseball games with you right in the middle of the action. You didn't care how old the players were or anything about their ability level. You just tried to make sure everyone had fun."

He was trying really hard to ignore the softness in her eyes and the warmth in her voice.

She had walked away from everything he wanted to offer her, without looking back. He had a right to be a little bitter, eight years later.

"So do you have any children?" she asked. She seemed genuinely interested, much to his surprise.

"One," he finally answered, not at all pleased with her line of questioning. He didn't like being reminded of old, tired dreams and newer failures.

"Boy or girl?"

"Boy. He's just turned five."

And he would be waiting impatiently for his father to pick him up if Richard didn't wrap things up quickly and escape.

"I do the best I can with him, especially since his mother and I aren't together anymore. The marriage ended right after he was born. I have full custody."

He wasn't sure why he added that. It wasn't something he just blurted out to people. If they hadn't been friends so long ago, he probably would have kept the information to himself.

Shock flickered in the depth of her blue eyes. "Oh. I hadn't heard that part. I'm so sorry, Richard."

He shrugged. "I'm sorry she's chosen to not be part of Ethan's life, but I'm not sorry about the divorce. It was one of those mistakes that make themselves painfully clear minutes after it's too late to be easily fixed."

"That doesn't make it hurt less, I would imagine," she murmured softly.

"No, it doesn't," he answered, his voice short. He regretted saying anything at all about Ethan and especially mentioning his failed marriage that still stung.

He gripped his briefcase, desperate to escape this awkwardness, but her words stopped him before he could do anything but put his hand on the doorknob.

"Can I ask you something?"

He eased his hand away, flashing her a wry look. "You haven't seemed to have any problem asking questions for the last two hours. You're amazingly good at it."

"That was different. Business. This is…not."

For the first time since the meeting she seemed to reveal her nerves weren't completely steel-coated. Wariness flickered in her eyes and she appeared to be gripping a file folder with inordinate force.

He ought to just push past her and get the hell out of there but he couldn't quite bring himself to move.

Instead, he shrugged. "Go ahead."

"I just wondered about this…hostility I'm sensing from you."

Apparently he wasn't as good at concealing his inner turmoil as he'd thought. "I'm sure you're imagining things."

"I don't think so," she answered, her voice pitched low. "I'm not an idiot, Richard."

Abruptly, suddenly, he was furious with her, as angry as he'd ever been with anyone. She had no right to come back, dredging up all these feelings he had buried long ago. The rejection, the hurt, the loss.

He had thrown his heart at her feet eight years ago. The hell of it was, he couldn't even say she had stomped on it. That might have been easier to handle, if she had shown any kind of malice.

But he supposed that would have been too much bother for her and would have required her to care a little. Instead, she had politely walked around it on her way out the door.

And then she dared to stand here now and ask him why he wasn't thrilled to see her!

This wasn't personal, he reminded himself. Or if some part of him couldn't help making it so, he shouldn't let everything between them become about their shared past. He couldn't afford it, not in his temporary role as hospital counsel.

"Why would I be hostile?" he said instead. "You're

only the point man—or woman, I guess—for a company trying to destroy this hospital and this community."

She blinked a little at his frontal assault, but it only took her seconds to recover. "Not true. I would have thought as an attorney you could look at this with a little more objectivity than…" Her voice trailed off.

"Than who? Your family?"

She sighed. "Yes. They won't listen to reason. Peter and David think I've betrayed the family name and Ella…well, Ella's not speaking to me at all."

He didn't expect the sympathy that suddenly tugged at him, fast on the heels of his own anger. Her family had always been important to her. Sometimes he thought she placed *too* much importance on their opinions. She had always seemed painfully aware that she was adopted and struggled hard to find a place for herself among the medicine-mad Wilders.

As a single child himself, he could only imagine what she must be feeling now—alienated by her siblings and bearing the brunt of their anger over her role in the NHC takeover attempt.

On the other hand, he instinctively sided with her siblings in this situation, not Anna.

He pushed away the wholly inappropriate urge to offer her comfort. "How did you expect them to react, Anna? This hospital is in their blood. Your family is basically the heart of Walnut River General. Everyone here knows that. And the soul, the essence, of this place is the sense of community—neighbors reaching out to help neighbors. That's what has made this hospital such an integral component to the quality of life in Walnut River. No one likes to go to the hospital, but the ordeal is made a little easier here when you know you'll be treated with respect and dignity, often by someone who has known you all your life."

She blinked with surprise. "Times change," she answered. "The health-care industry is changing. Independent community hospitals just don't have the competitive edge anymore."

"Nor should they. It's not about making money. It's about helping people heal."

"Exactly! And if Northeastern HealthCare can help them heal in a more efficient, cost-effective way and provide better access to cutting-edge procedures not currently available in this market, don't you think that will be better for everyone in the long run?"

"Will it?"

"Yes!" she exclaimed. "Walnut River would be part of a powerful consortium of health-care providers. With that backing, the hospital can afford to bring in state-of-the-art equipment and the newest procedures. NHC is already talking about building a cancer treatment center so patients don't have to drive twenty miles away for radiation treatment! And they're talking about an entire renovation of the labor and delivery unit and an after-hours Instacare facility for parents who work during the day to bring their children to see a doctor...."

Her voice trailed off and color brushed her cheeks like the first hint of autumn on the maple trees along the river. "I didn't mean to ramble on. I'm afraid I get a little... passionate sometimes."

She obviously believed the NHC takeover would truly be best for the hospital. Richard had to admire her passion, even if he disagreed with it.

"You certainly are free to believe what you want," he said. "And I'll do the same."

After a moment, she nodded. "Fair enough. But that doesn't really answer my question."

"What question would that be?"

She opened her mouth to answer but before she could, the boardroom door opened and Tina Tremaine, J.D.'s receptionist, stepped through.

"Oh. I'm sorry. I thought everyone was gone."

"We're just on our way out," Richard answered.

"You don't have to rush. Take your time. I only needed to make sure things were straightened up in here for a meeting J.D. has first thing in the morning."

She smiled at Richard but he was surprised to see her smile disappear completely by the time she turned to Anna.

Anna didn't seem to miss the sudden disdain in the other woman's eyes. Her shoulders straightened and her chin tilted up slightly but she said nothing.

"We're just leaving," Richard said again.

"Fine." Tina closed the door behind her, leaving behind a sudden awkward silence.

"Look, would you like to go somewhere? Grab an early dinner or something?" Anna asked.

He gazed at her, stunned that some tiny part of him was actually tempted, even though the more rational part of his brain recognized the absurdity of the impulse.

"That's not a good idea, Anna."

Somewhere in the depths of her blue eyes he thought he saw a shadow of vulnerability, just the barest hint of loneliness. But she mustered a brittle-looking smile. "Really? Why not? What could possibly be the harm in it? We're just two old friends catching up over dinner."

"Two old friends who happen to be standing on opposite sides of a corporate battlefield."

"Oh, for heaven's sake. That doesn't mean we can't be civil to each other! You were one of my closest friends, Richard. I told you things no one else in the world knows about me."

You said you loved me and then you walked away when something better came along.

His bitterness again seemed to sweep up out of nowhere, taking him completely by surprise.

He thought he had dealt with all this years ago. He never would have guessed seeing her would dredge up all those feelings and make them fresh and raw all over again.

He chose his words carefully, not at all eager to reveal too much to her. "I'm sorry, Anna. Even if not for the gray area regarding conflict of interest ethics in seeing you socially, I have other plans."

She froze for an instant and color climbed her cheeks. "Some other time then, perhaps. It was…great to see you again."

She headed for the walnut-paneled door. As she reached out to pull it open, he thought she paused slightly. Her gaze met his and if he hadn't known her so well years ago, he probably would have missed the flash of trepidation there.

He wondered at it for only an instant before he realized what must lie beneath her hesitation. Judging by Tina's reaction in the boardroom just now, he was willing to bet Anna wasn't at all popular at Walnut River General Hospital. The antimerger forces were vocal and vociferous in their opposition.

Again that unwanted sympathy surged through him.

He might not agree with her position but he couldn't argue with her convictions. She was only doing her job and she didn't deserve to be mistreated by employees of the hospital who might oppose her mission here.

"I'll walk out with you," he said impulsively.

Her lush, delectable mouth opened a little with surprise, then she rewarded him with a glowing smile that made him far too aware of how the years between them had only added to her loveliness.

Much to his dismay, he suddenly felt a familiar clutch of desire twist his insides. He wanted to reach across the space between them and capture that mouth with his, to see if her skin was as silky as he remembered, if she still tasted heady and sweet.

He had been far too long without a woman. Between Ethan and trying to build his practice, he had little time or inclination left for extracurricular activity.

Maybe he needed to make time—especially since the one woman who stirred his interest in longer than he cared to remember was. Anna Wilder.

It was ridiculous for her to be so grateful Richard was walking beside her. What did she expect, that she would need a bodyguard to help her safely make it through the hospital?

She might be persona non grata around the hospital right now, but she couldn't quite believe anyone would physically assault her to keep NHC at bay.

Still, she couldn't deny she found great comfort from Richard's calm presence as they headed for the elevator. She always had, she remembered now. He had been a source of strength and comfort through high school and college—the one she always turned to for advice, for counsel, for encouragement.

And more.

She pushed the memories away, refusing to dwell on them. She couldn't think about them right now, when he was only a few feet away looking blond and dangerously gorgeous.

They paused at the elevator to wait for a car and stood in silence, watching the numbers rise. She was just about to ask him about his other clients when she heard a commotion down the hall.

"Hold the elevator. The trauma lift isn't working."

Anna sucked in her breath as the familiar voice rang through the hallway. Her insides knotted with dread but she had no choice but to turn her head.

She wasn't at all surprised to see her sister working an oxygen pump as a team of medical personnel pushed a gurney down the hall. Anna had a quick impression that the patient was a middle-aged woman with her face covered in blood.

Ella faltered for just a moment when she saw Anna but she didn't break her stride. "Have the ER hold trauma room one," she told a nurse running beside them. "And alert the surgical team that we've got a femoral compound fracture and possible head trauma."

She snapped out other commands firmly in a crisp, focused tone that reminded Anna painfully of their father, leaving no doubt exactly who was in charge of the situation.

She had never seen her sister in a professional capacity, Anna realized, as a mixture of pride and awe washed through her.

She always knew Ella would kick butt as a doctor. Seeing her in action was all the confirmation she needed. Ella was cool, composed and completely in control—all the things Anna couldn't quite manage during her single year of med school.

Anna and Richard stepped aside to allow the team access to the elevator. Just before the doors slid closed, Anna's gaze met her sister's for only a millisecond.

Everything on the periphery seemed to fade, and for a moment Anna was ten years old again, snuggling in her sleeping bag in a tent in their big backyard next to her sister and best friend while the stars popped out, sharing secrets and popcorn and dreams.

Oh, Ella. I miss you so much, she wanted to whisper, but she could never say the words tangled in her throat, and in an instant, the doors closed and the moment was gone.

She fought back tears, praying her emotions wouldn't betray her in front of Richard.

"Wow," he said after a moment. "Hurricane Ella, as usual."

"Right." She didn't trust herself to say more than that as a thousand different regrets pinched at her.

Their rift was largely her fault, one that had been widening for eight years since she left Walnut River, and it had become an unbreachable chasm these days.

If she had told Ella and their brothers about her job with NHC, her involvement in the merger might not have come as such a shock to the other Wilders. Instead, for two long years she had chosen the coward's way, avoiding their questions when they asked about her work, offering them half-truths and evasions.

She had suspected exactly how they would react.

She supposed that was the reason she had deceived them for so long.

"Not a good time for sisterly conversation, obviously."

She wrenched her mind away from her guilt to Richard, who was watching her with entirely too much perception in his blue eyes.

She forced a smile past her aching heart. "Ella runs a mile a minute. She always has. When we were kids, she was always on the go. You remember what she was like."

"I do. There was never a quiet moment with the two Wilder girls around."

She forced another smile, though she had a feeling it was probably as transparent as it felt. She could only hope he didn't see the hurt washing through her in fierce waves.

"You never asked your question," he said.

She blinked at him. "Sorry. What question was that?"

"I don't know. You said you wanted to ask me something and then we were sidetracked."

She frowned, replaying their conversation of the past few minutes in her mind. Suddenly she remembered the direction of her thoughts and she could feel herself flush.

If not for the encounter with Ella, she might have made some laughing remark and changed the subject. But her emotions were too raw for equivocation and for some strange reason she decided to be blunt.

"I did ask you, but you didn't give me a straight answer. I'm just wondering if it's business or personal."

"What?"

"The…hostility. Coolness, antipathy, whatever you want to call it. I'm just wondering if you're angry because I work for NHC or if there's something else behind it."

A strange light flickered in his eyes for just an instant

before his handsome features became a mask once more. He opened his mouth but before he could say anything, the elevator arrived.

Only after they stepped inside and he pushed the button to return to the main floor did he turn to answer her.

"I suppose a little of both," he said. "We were friends. You said it yourself. And for one night, we were far more than that. I guess I'm trying to figure out how a woman I considered a friend could turn her back on her family and this town."

I didn't, she wanted to cry. But she was already so tired of defending herself and her choices to everyone in Walnut River. Didn't anyone think it was possible—just maybe—that she might have the community's best interests at heart?

Richard certainly didn't. She could see the censure in his eyes. She couldn't argue with him. That was the hell of it. He had the right to his opinions and she suspected nothing she said would convince him her motives were anything other than crass profit.

The elevator arrived at the main floor and the doors sprang open. He walked with her through the lobby, past the censorious eyes and out of the hospital.

She wanted to thank him for providing a buffer, but she couldn't figure out just how to put the words together.

"I'm parked over there," he pointed.

"Oh. I'm on the other side. I guess I'll see you around, then."

"Probably not. I was only filling in temporarily today in the meeting. My partner is usually the one at our firm who represents the hospital. He should be back on the job tomorrow."

She should be relieved, she told herself. The prospect of spending more time with this prickly, distant Richard who had once been so very dear to her was not appealing.

"Well, in that case, it was…good to see you today."

"Right," he answered.

She walked to her car, wondering why she felt worse leaving the hospital than she had going in.

Chapter Three

Twenty minutes later, Anna walked into her duplex apartment and was instantly assaulted by a miniature dynamo.

Her dark mood instantly lifted as if dozens of sunbeams had followed her home.

"There's my Lilli-girl."

Her tiny dog gave one short yip of greeting then did a standing leap on all four legs, jumping almost to Anna's knees. She laughed at the dog's antics and bent to scoop Lilli into her arms, all five pounds of her.

"Did you have a good day, sweetheart? I hope those two big monsters didn't run you ragged."

Lilli—short for Lilliputian—yipped again and wriggled in her arms maneuvering so she could lick eagerly at Anna's chin with her tiny sandpaper tongue.

Anna smiled and cuddled the dog closer. What a blessing this duplex had turned out to be, one of the few bright spots in her life since she had been ordered by the NHC CEO, Alfred Daly to come home to Walnut River to wrap up the hospital merger.

She hadn't been able to find a single hotel in town that would allow pets, but then she'd stumbled on this furnished place near the river that would allow a temporary lease for the short time she expected to be in Walnut River.

The duplex itself wasn't anything fancy, just bare bones lodging with little personality or style. But it had a good-sized backyard for Lilli to play in, and the landlady had two gentle yellow labradors who already adored her little Chihuahua-pug mix and kept her company all day.

Yeah, Anna was paying an arm and a leg above her per diem for the few weeks she expected to be here. But she figured it was worth it if she didn't have to kennel Lilli during her time in Walnut River or confuse her with a temporary placement with one of her friends or coworkers back in Manhattan.

She adored the dog and had from the moment she heard her tiny whimpering squeaks from a Dumpster near her subway stop in the financial district. Anna had been on her way back uptown on a cold dank January evening after working late and only heard the puppy by a fluke when she had paused for a moment to fix a broken heel on her shoe.

Another night, she might have been in too big a rush to investigate the sound. But that night, something had sparked her curiosity and she had dug through the Dumpster until she found Lilli, bedraggled, flea-infested, half-starved. The tiny puppy had looked at her with pleading dark eyes and Anna had been lost.

That had been six months before, just after her father

died. She freely admitted that while dog ownership had been an adjustment, especially with her hectic schedule and the added complications of city life, she had never once regretted her decision to rescue the puppy. Lilli had brought boundless happiness into her world.

Not that her life hadn't been fulfilling before, she reminded herself. She had carved out a comfortable life for herself in New York. She enjoyed her job and found it challenging and interesting. She had good friends in the city, she volunteered at an after-school mentoring program, she enjoyed a full and active social life.

Still, somewhere deep in her heart, she sometimes yearned for the comfortable pace and quiet serenity of Walnut River and she couldn't deny that she missed her family, especially Ella.

She remembered the heated anger that had flashed in her sister's eyes earlier at the hospital and hugged Lilli a little closer to her. She had ruined her chance for any kind of reconciliation with her family by deceiving them for two years.

Understanding and accepting her own culpability in the situation somehow didn't make it any easier to endure.

She sighed. "I need a good ride to clear my head. What do you say, Lilli-girl?"

The dog gave a yip of approval and Anna smiled and set her down, then hurried into her temporary bedroom. The dog followed on her heels, then danced around the room impatiently as Anna changed from her business suit to lycra bike shorts and a matching shirt. The transformation only took a few moments, with a few more needed to change her work chignon to a more practical ponytail.

A short time later, they set off with Lilli in her safety

harness, watching the world pass from her perch inside a custom-made basket on the front of Anna's racing bike.

Almost instantly, Anna felt some of the tension leave her shoulders. Even in the city, this was her escape, riding along her favorite trails in Central Park, exploring new neighborhoods, darting around taxis and buses.

Rediscovering the streets of her hometown had been a particular pleasure these past few days, and she could feel herself relax as the bike's tires hummed along the asphalt.

Early summer had to be her favorite time of year, she decided, when the world was green and lovely. As she rode down one street and then another, she savored the smells and sights, so different from her life the past eight years in Manhattan.

The evening air was thick with the sweet smell of flowers, of meat grilling on a barbecue somewhere, of freshly mowed lawns.

She pushed herself hard, making a wide circuit around the edge of town before circling back. By the time she cut through the park near her duplex, she felt much more centered and better equipped to tackle the mounds of paperwork still awaiting her attention that evening.

The trail through the park took her past a baseball diamond where a game was underway. Because it seemed like such a perfect ending to her ride, a great way to celebrate a June evening, she paused to watch for a moment in the dying rays of the sun.

The players were young. She had never been very good at gauging children's ages but since many of them still had their baby fat and seemed more interested in jabbering to each other than paying attention to the game, she would have guessed them at five or so.

She smiled, watching one eager batter swing at the ball on the tee a half-dozen times before he finally connected. The ball sailed into right field, just past a player who ran after it on stubby little legs.

"Run for it, bud. You can catch it. That's the way."

Anna jerked her head around at the voice ringing from the stands and stood frozen with dismay.

When Richard claimed another commitment, she had assumed he meant a date. Instead, he sat in the bleachers looking gorgeous and casual in jeans and a golf shirt, cheering on the towheaded little outfielder she assumed was his son.

For just an instant, she was tempted to ride away quickly so he didn't think she was stalking him or something, but Lilli chose that inopportune moment to yip from her perch in the basket.

Drawn to the sound, Richard turned his head and she saw his eyes widen with surprise as he recognized her.

For one breathless instant, she thought she saw something else flicker there, something hot. But it was gone so quickly she was certain she must have imagined it.

She raised a hand in greeting and then—mostly because she didn't know what else to do amid the awkwardness of the chance encounter—she climbed from her bicycle, propped it against the metal bleachers then scooped Lilli out of the basket before joining him in the stands.

"That must be Ethan out there," she said.

"It is. We're up one run with one out and just need to hold them through this inning and it will be all over."

He turned his attention back to the game in time to cheer as the next player at bat hit the ball straight at the shortstop, who tossed it to first base. The fielder on first base looked astonished that he actually caught the ball in time to pick off the runner.

"I have to admit, I'm a little surprised to see you here," Richard said after a moment when the crowd's wild cheers subsided. "I wouldn't have expected a T-ball game to be quite up your alley."

Anna gave a rueful smile. "I only stopped on a whim. We live just a block away from here and have ridden through the park several times. This is the first game I've stopped at."

"We?"

She held up Lilli and Richard raised one of his elegant eyebrows. "Is that a dog or a rat with a bad case of indigestion?"

She made a face. "Hey, watch it. This is the queen of my heart. Lilli, this is Richard Green. Say hi."

The dog deigned to lift her paw but Richard only blinked. "You're kidding."

Anna shook her head, hiding a smile. "I'm afraid not. She'll be offended if you don't shake."

With a sigh, he reached out a hand to take the dog's tiny paw in his, which was all the encouragement Lilli needed to decide he was her new best friend. She wriggled with delight and gazed at him out of adoring eyes.

This wasn't the first time Anna had noticed her dog had a weakness for handsome men.

"So you said the center fielder is your son?"

Richard nodded. "He's the one picking dandelions," he said wryly.

Anna laughed. "Correct me if I'm wrong, but I see three kids picking dandelions out there."

He smiled and she wondered how she could possibly

have forgotten the devastating impact of his smile. "Mine's the one in the middle."

As if on cue, the center fielder began to wave vigorously. "Hi, Daddy! Can you see me?"

Richard nodded. "I see you, buddy," he called out. "Watch the ball, okay?"

Ethan beamed at his father and obeyed, turning his attention back to the game just in time as a pop fly headed straight for him.

"Right there!" Richard exclaimed. "You can do it!"

Ethan held his glove out so far from his face it seemed to dangle from his wrist but the ball somehow miraculously landed right in the sweet spot with a solid thud.

Caught up in the moment, Anna jumped to her feet cheering with delight, along with Richard and the rest of the onlookers on their side of the bleachers.

"That's the game," the umpire called. "Final score, sixteen to fifteen."

Anna held tight to Lilli as the little dog picked up on the excitement of the crowd, yipped with glee and vibrated in her arms, desperate to be part of the action.

"Great game," she said after a moment. "Be sure to tell Ethan congratulations for me."

"I'll do that. Or it looks like you can tell him that yourself. Here he comes."

An instant later, a small figure rushed toward them, his features bright with excitement as he launched himself at his father.

"Did you see that, Dad? I caught the ball right in my glove! Right in my glove! I won the game! Did you see?"

Richard hugged his son with enthusiasm. "Nice work! I'm so proud of you, bud. You're getting better every game."

"I know. I am." He said it with such blatant confidence that Anna couldn't help but smile.

Lilli, never one to sit quietly when hugs were being exchanged and someone else was getting attention she thought rightfully belonged to her, gave another of her love-me yips and the boy quickly turned toward her.

"Wow! Is that your dog?" he exclaimed to Anna, the baseball game apparently forgotten.

Anna set Lilli down, careful to hold on to the retractable leash while Lilli trotted eagerly to the boy. He instantly scooped her into his arms and giggled with delight when the dog licked the little-boy sweat from his cheek.

"What's his name?" Ethan asked eagerly.

"She's a girl and her name is Lilli," Anna answered.

"I like her!"

She smiled, charmed by how much this darling boy resembled his father. "I do, too. She's a great dog."

"My name is Ethan Richard Green. What's yours?"

She sent a swift look toward Richard, not at all sure if he would approve of her engaging in a long conversation with her son. He returned her questioning look with an impassive one of his own, which she took as tacit approval for her to answer.

"My name is Anna. Anna Wilder. Your dad and I knew each other a long time ago."

"Hi." He set Lilli on the ground carefully and held out a polite hand to her, a gesture that charmed her all over again.

She shook it solemnly, tumbling head over heels in love with the little boy.

"I'm very pleased to meet you, Miss Wilder," he said, obviously reciting a lesson drummed into him by someone.

"And I'm very pleased to meet you as well, Mr. Green," she answered in the same vein.

His solemnity didn't last long, apparently, at least not with Lilli around. He knelt to pet the dog, giggling as she tried to lick him again.

"Would you like to hold her leash?" Anna asked.

"Can I?"

"If it's okay with your dad."

Ethan looked at his father, who nodded. "You can take her once around the bleachers but don't go farther than that."

The little boy gripped the leash handle tightly and the two of them headed away.

"I wouldn't have pegged you for a dog person," Richard said after a moment.

"Why not?"

"I don't know. Just seems like a lot of responsibility for a single executive living in the big city."

Though his words echoed her own thoughts of earlier in the evening, she still bristled a little that he apparently doubted she might possess the necessary nurturing abilities.

"It's not always easy, but I make it work," she answered. "What about you? I wouldn't have pegged you for Little League games and car-pool duty. Talk about responsibility, Mr. High-Powered Attorney."

One corner of his mouth quirked into a smile. "Point taken. Just like you, it's not always easy but I make it work."

She didn't doubt it was a major juggling act—nor did she doubt Richard handled it with his typical elegant competence, just as she remembered him doing everything.

Both of them turned to watch Ethan and Lilli make

their way through other onlookers and players back around the bleachers.

Richard sighed as the boy and dog approached. "You know this is going to be one more salvo in our ongoing, occasionally virulent we-need-a-puppy debate."

She laughed at his woeful tone. "Sorry to cause more trouble for you. But Ethan is welcome to borrow Lilli anytime he'd like while I'm still in Walnut River."

He looked less than thrilled at the prospect, which only made her smile widen.

"That was super fun," Ethan exclaimed. "Can I do it again?"

"You'd better give Lilli back to Anna now, bud. Remember what I promised you after the game?"

"Oh yeah!" He handed the leash over to Anna. "We're gonna get a shaved ice," he exclaimed. "My dad promised I could have one if I was a good sport and didn't get mad if I didn't get on base again. Hey, do you and Lilli want a shaved ice, too?"

She slanted a look at Richard, who was again wearing that impassive mask.

Common sense told her to pick up her dog and run. She didn't need to spend more time with either of the Green males, both of whom she found enormously appealing on entirely different levels.

On the other hand, all that awaited her at her place was more paperwork. And she couldn't escape the sudden conviction that Richard wanted her to say no, which conversely made her want to do exactly the opposite.

"I'd love a shaved ice," she proclaimed. "It's thirsty work carrying a huge dog like Lilli around. Wears me right out."

The boy giggled as he eyed the miniscule Chihuahua. "You're super funny, Miss Wilder."

She hadn't heard that particular sentiment in a long, long time. She couldn't remember the last time anyone had thought she was anything other than a boring numbers-cruncher. She decided she liked it.

"You know what? You can call me Anna, as long as I can call you Ethan. Is that okay?"

"Sure."

"Ethan, would you mind holding Lilli's leash while I walk my bike?"

He nodded eagerly. "I won't let go, I promise," he said.

"Okay. I trust you."

She slanted one more look at Richard, who was watching their exchange with only a slight tightening of his mouth showing his displeasure. She almost apologized for forcing herself into a family event but then gave a mental shrug.

They were only sharing shaved ices, not spending the entire evening together.

This was completely unfair.

Richard barely had time to adjust to the idea that she was back in town and here she was again, crowding his space, intruding in his carefully constructed life, making him think about things he had put on the back burner.

A casual observer probably wouldn't be able to imagine that the coolly competent executive he had spent two hours with earlier in the day could be the same woman as this softer, far more approachable, version.

This Anna looked sleek and trim and sexy as hell, with all that gorgeous blond hair pulled back in a ponytail and her skin glowing with vitality.

She looked much like he remembered his old friend from eight years ago—bright and vibrant and so beautiful he couldn't manage to look away for longer than a minute or two at a time.

She seemed completely oblivious to her allure as she walked beside him, pushing her bike. And he would have bet she had no idea how hard it was for him to fight down the surge of pure lust.

The evening was one of those beautiful Walnut River summer evenings and the park was full of families taking advantage of it. He greeted several people he knew on the short walk to the shaved ice stand but didn't stop to talk with any of them.

"Do you know every single person in town?" Anna asked after a few minutes.

"Not quite. There are some new apartment complexes on the other side of town and I believe there one or two tenants there're I haven't managed to meet yet. I'm working on it, though."

He meant it as a joke but she apparently didn't quite catch the humor. "Are you running for mayor or something?"

He gave a rough laugh. "Me? Not quite. I've just lived here most of my life. You can't help but come to know a lot of people when you're part of a community."

"Why did you stick around Walnut River?" she asked him. "You always had such big plans when you were in law school. You were going to head out to the wild frontier somewhere, open your own practice and work on changing the world one client at a time."

He remembered those plans. He had dreamed of heading out West. Colorado, maybe, or Utah. Somewhere with outdoor opportunities like skiing and mountain biking—all the things he didn't have time to do now that he was a single father.

"Things change. Life never quite turns out like we expect when we're twenty-two, does it?"

He didn't think he had ever confided in her the rest of those dreams. He had been desperately in love with Anna Wilder and wanted to bundle her up and take her into the wilderness with him.

She was quiet, her eyes on his son, who was giggling at her little rat-dog. "Maybe not. But sometimes it's better, though, isn't it?"

The fading rays of the sun caught in Ethan's blond hair and Richard's heart twisted with love for his son.

"Absolutely." He paused. "And to answer your question about why I'm still here, mostly it's because this is where my mother lives. She takes Ethan most days when I'm working and they're crazy about each other. She's a godsend."

"Is Ethan's mother in the picture at all?"

He wasn't sure he could honestly say Lynne had ever really been in the picture. Their relationship had been a mistake from the beginning and he suspected they both would have figured that out if not for her accidental pregnancy that had precipitated their marriage.

"Is that the wrong question?" Anna asked quietly and he realized he had been silent for just a hair too long.

"No. It's fine. The short answer is no. The long answer is a bit more...complex."

He wasn't about to go into the long and ugly story with Anna, about how Lynne hadn't wanted children in the first place, how she had become pregnant during their last year of law school together, that she probably would have had an abortion if she hadn't been raised strict Catholic.

Instead, he had talked her into marrying him.

Though she had tried hard for the first few months after Ethan was born, Lynne had been a terrible mother—impatient, easily frustrated, not at all nurturing to an infant who needed so much more.

It had been better all the way around when she accepted a job overseas.

"I'm sorry," Anna said again. "I didn't mean to dredge up something painful."

"It's not. Not really."

She didn't look as if she believed him, but by then they had reached the shaved ice stand. Ethan was waiting for them, jumping around in circles with the same enthusiasm as Anna's little dog as he waited impatiently for them to arrive.

"I want Tiger's Blood, just like I always have," Ethan declared.

Richard shook his head. His son rarely had anything else but the tropical fruit flavor. "You need to try a different kind once in awhile, kiddo."

"I like Tiger's Blood," he insisted.

"Same here," Anna agreed. "You know what's weird? It's Lilli's favorite flavor, too. I think it's the whole dog-cat thing. Makes her feel like a big, bad tough guy."

Though Ethan looked puzzled, Richard felt a laugh bubble out as he looked at her tiny dog prancing around at the end of her leash.

His gaze met Anna's and for just an instant, he felt like he was back in high school, making stupid jokes and watching movies together and wondering if he would ever find the courage to tell the prettiest girl in school he was crazy about her.

They weren't in high school anymore, he reminded himself sternly. She might still be the prettiest girl he had ever seen but he certainly wasn't crazy about her anymore. The years between them had taken care of that, and he wasn't about to change the status quo.

Chapter Four

The line was remarkably short and they had their icy treats only a few moments later.

"I saw a bench over there," Anna said. "Do you want to sit down?"

Richard knew he ought to just gather up his son and head home. But he couldn't quite force himself to sever this fragile connection between them, though he knew damn well it was a mistake to spend more time with her.

He was largely silent while they ate the shaved ice. For that matter, so was Anna, who seemed content to listen to Ethan chatter about his friends in kindergarten, his new two-wheel bike, the kind of puppy he wanted if his dad would ever agree.

Though Richard wondered how he could possibly have time to eat around all the never-ending chatter, Ethan finished his shaved ice in about five minutes flat then begged to play on the playground conveniently located next to the stand.

"Not for long, okay? It's been a long day and you need to get home and into the tub."

Ethan made a face as he handed Lilli's leash back to Anna then raced off toward the slide.

"He seems like a great kid," Anna said after a moment.

"He is. Seeing the world through his eyes helps keep my life in perspective."

"He's lucky to have you for a father."

She paused, her eyes shadowed. "My dad's been gone for six months and I still can't believe it."

Her father's opinion had always been important to Anna. Maybe too important.

He had respected her father—everyone in town had. James Wilder had been a brilliant, compassionate physician who had saved countless lives during his decades of practicing medicine in Walnut River. He doubted there was a family in town that didn't have some member who had been treated by Dr. Wilder.

But he didn't necessarily agree with the way James had treated his children. Even when they were younger Richard had seen how James singled Anna out, how hard he tried to include her in everything and make her feel an integral part of the family.

From an outsider's standpoint, Richard thought James's efforts only seemed to isolate Anna more, reminding her constantly that she was different by virtue of her adoption and fostering resentment and antipathy in her siblings.

"I tried to find you at the funeral to offer my condolences but you must have left early."

She set her plastic spoon back in the cup, her features suddenly tight. "It was a hard day all the way around. My father's death was such a shock to me and I'm afraid I didn't handle things well. I couldn't wait to get out of there and return to New York so I could... could grieve."

He found it inexpressibly sad that she hadn't wanted to turn to her siblings during their moment of shared sorrow.

"Have you seen Peter or David since you've been back?"

"No. Only Ella, today at the hospital." Her brittle smile didn't conceal the hurt in her eyes. "I'm quite sure they're all going out of their way to avoid me."

"They may not even be aware you're back in town."

"You know better than that, Richard. They know I'm here."

She was quiet for a moment, then offered that forced smile again. "It's not exactly a secret that NHC has sent me here to close the merger after six months of problems. I might not have received an angry phone call from holier-than-thou Peter or a snide, sarcastic email from David, but they know I'm here."

He didn't want to feel this soft sympathy for her but he couldn't seem to keep it from welling up, anyway.

She had created the situation, he reminded himself sternly. Why should he feel sorry for her at the estrangement with her siblings when she had done everything possible to stir up their wrath?

She shrugged. "Anyway, I'm sure J.D. spread the word he was meeting with me today."

She rose suddenly and threw her half-eaten shaved ice in the garbage can next to their bench. He had the distinct impression she regretted letting her emotions filter through.

"Which reminds me, I'd better go. I've got a great deal of paperwork to file after today's meeting."

He didn't think the reminder of their adversarial roles in the takeover was at all accidental.

She picked up her little dog and set her in a carrier attached to the handlebars of her bike. In bike shorts that hugged her trim, athletic figure, she looked long and lovely and so delectable she made his mouth water.

"It was nice bumping into you and meeting Ethan. Thank you for letting me share a little of your evening together."

"You're welcome."

She gave him one more small smile then, to his surprise, she stopped at the playground to say goodbye to Ethan. She even went so far as to take the dog out of her carrier one last time so the petite creature could lick at Ethan's face.

Their interaction touched something deep inside him. In his experience, most women either completely ignored his son or went over the top in their attentions, fawning all over Ethan in an effort to convince Richard how maternal they could be.

Anna's interest in Ethan seemed genuine—and it was obvious his son was smitten by her.

Or at least by her little rat-dog.

After a moment she gave Ethan one last high five, settled Lilli in her carrier again and rode away with one last wave to both of them.

He watched her go—as he had watched her go before. He sighed, his mind on that last miserable day when she had left Walnut River.

He still wasn't sure exactly why the hell she had left— or, more importantly, why the memory of it still stung.

They had been good friends through high school and he could admit to himself now that he'd always had a bit of a crush on her, though he hadn't fully realized it until college.

They went to different universities for their undergraduate work. He was at Harvard, but since she had only been a few miles away at Radcliffe, they had seen each other often, but still only as friends.

Though he could sense his feelings for her deepening and growing, they had both been running in opposite directions. He was headed for law school while she was busy preparing for med school.

But one summer night after their first year of graduate work everything had changed.

By a happy coincidence, they had both been home in Walnut River temporarily for the wedding of a friend. Since neither of them had dates, they had decided to go together—again, strictly as friends.

But he had taken one look at her in a sleek, pale-blue dress he could still remember vividly and he hadn't been able to look away.

They had danced every dance together at the wedding reception and by the time the night was over, he'd realized he had been hiding the truth from himself all those years.

He was in love with her

Deeply, ferociously in love.

And she had returned his feelings—or least, she had given a good imitation of it.

After the wedding festivities were over, they had gone to his house for a late-night swim. His parents were gone and he and Anna had stayed up long into the night, sharing confidences and heady kisses, holding hands while they looked at the stars and savored being together.

And then they had made love and he still remembered it as the single most moving experience of his life, except for Ethan's birth. She had given him her innocence and had told him she was falling in love with him.

And then in the morning, everything had changed.

The memory seemed permanently imprinted into his head, of standing on the front porch of her parents' house just hours after he had left her there, those stars still in his eyes.

He'd expected to find the woman he had just realized he loved.

Instead, he'd found chaos. Anna was gone. She must have left soon after he had dropped her at her doorstep, with one, last, long, lingering kiss and the promise of many more.

Both of her brothers were living away from home at the time but Richard clearly remembered the reaction of the three remaining Wilders. Her father had been devastated, her mother baffled and Ella had been crushed.

He couldn't really say she had left without a word. She'd mailed him a letter that had arrived the next day— a terse, emotionless thing.

What kind of fool was he that he could still remember the damn thing word for word?

Dear Richard.

I can't do this with you right now. I'm so sorry. I meant everything I said last night about my feelings for you, but after I've had a few hours to think about it, I realize I can't string you along while I try to figure out my life. It wouldn't be fair to you and to be honest, I'm not sure I have the emotional strength for it. You deserve so much more.

I have to go, Richard. I can't live this lie anymore. Being with you last night only showed me that more clearly. I'm being crushed by the weight of my family's expectations and I don't know any other way to break free of them. I only wish, more than anything, that I didn't have to hurt you in the process.

She had signed it with love and, while he had wanted to believe her, she had made no other effort to contact him.

That had been eight years ago. Another lifetime. Then had come Lynne and Ethan and his world had changed once more.

But his heart had never forgotten her.

He sighed, acknowledging the truth of that rather grim realization.

Some part of him still had feelings for Anna Wilder, feelings he didn't dare take out and examine right now.

It was a damn good thing his partner was representing Walnut River General in the whole NHC matter.

Richard wasn't sure his heart—or his ego—could handle being screwed over by Anna Wilder again.

Two days later, Richard sat in his office rubbing the bridge of his nose and trying to fight back the odd sensation that the walls of his office had suddenly shrunk considerably.

"Say that again. Where are you, Phil?"

His partner gave a heavy sigh, sounding not at all like his normal affable self. "Wyoming, at the Clear Springs Rehab Center. It's supposed to be one of the best in the nation."

"Rehab, Phil? Is this some kind of sick joke?"

"I wish it were that easy."

"I'm stunned!"

"You shouldn't be," the other man said wearily. "You covered for me enough the last six months that you should have seen the clues. Peggy's gone. She moved out two weeks ago and took the kids with her."

Those walls seemed to crowd a few inches closer. "You didn't say a word to me!"

"What was I going to say? I was too ashamed. My wife left me, my kids aren't talking to me. I've only held it together at work by luck and a hell of a good partner."

Okay, Richard had to admit he had suspected something was going on. With all the sick days and missed meetings, he had wondered if Phil was fighting a serious illness he wasn't ready to disclose.

In retrospect, he wondered how the hell he possibly could have missed the signs.

"I'm an alcoholic, Richard. I can't hide it anymore. I've tried to stop a dozen times on my own and I can't. This is the only way I know how to straighten out my life."

All the pieces seemed to fall into place with a hard thunk and again Richard wondered where his own head had been to miss something so glaring in his partner and friend.

Yeah, there had been mistakes the past few months—a couple of serious ones that Richard had been forced to step in and mend. But he had just assumed Phil would tell him what was going on when he was ready. He hadn't minded the clean-up work. Phil had been a mentor and a friend since he came to the practice straight out of law school, green in more than name and a single father of an infant to boot.

"How long will you be there?" he finally asked.

"As long as it takes. I wish I could be more specific

than that but I don't know at this point. The average stay is two months."

Two months? Richard fought down a groan. They had too much work as it was and had discussed adding another partner to the practice to help ease the burden.

"What about your clients?" he asked.

"I'm sorry to dump them on you. But my two junior associates have been basically carrying everything for the last few months, anyway. They can bring you up to speed on the major cases. I'm not worried about anything but the hospital takeover attempt. I'm afraid you'll have to step in and handle that. My files are copious, though. You should find everything you need there."

"I'll take care of everything on this end," Richard assured him. "You just focus on what you're doing there."

"Thanks, man. Entering into a partnership with you was the smartest move I've made in years."

Richard hung up a few moments later and let out a long, slow breath. He was concerned about his friend, first and foremost. But he was also suddenly overwhelmed with the weight of more responsibilities.

The hospital merger had been Phil's project for six months. Richard had helped a little but getting up to speed on all the intricate details was going to take days, if not weeks.

Talk about a complication. Just when he was thinking he wouldn't have to have anything more to do with Anna Wilder, circumstances had to go and change dramatically.

He would have no choice now but to work with her, on a much closer level than he was sure made him completely comfortable, given their shared past.

* * *

Amazing how a day could go from rough to truly miserable in the space of a few moments.

Anna stood in the cafeteria line in the basement of Walnut River General, wondering why she was even bothering to grab a salad when her appetite had abruptly fled and the idea of trying to force down lunch was about as appealing as walking back through the halls of the hospital and encountering another of her testy siblings.

She sighed, moving her tray along the metal track, one step closer to the cashier.

Blast David anyway.

Of all her siblings, she would have expected him to at least be civil to her—not because they had been the best of friends but because she had a tough time thinking he would bother to involve himself in the political side of things at the hospital.

Peter had at least tried to be brotherly to her, but because he was so much older than she, their lives had always seemed on slightly different tracks.

Ella had been closest to her, in age and in their relationship. If not for the distance she herself had placed between them after she dropped out of medical school and moved away from Walnut River, she imagined she and her sister would still have been close.

David, though, had always seemed a challenge. She'd always had the vague sense that he resented her. He had never been deliberately cruel, had just treated her with somewhat chilly indifference, making it overtly obvious he didn't want to be bothered with a whiny little sister who wasn't even really related to him.

She supposed nothing had really changed. Rather

blindly, she pushed her tray one person closer to the cashier, replaying the scene outside the cafeteria doors just a few moments earlier.

After spending all morning going over records the hospital refused to allow her to take off-site, she had been tempted to go somewhere in town for lunch. Maybe Prudy's Menu downtown or a fast-food place somewhere.

But since she was looking at several more hours of analyzing patient accounts, she had decided to save time by eating in the cafeteria.

Big mistake. She should have considered the possibility that she might encounter one of her testy siblings.

Sure enough, when she reached the cafeteria, the first person she had seen had been David, looking relaxed and happier than she'd seen him in a long time.

Becoming engaged and moving back to Walnut River apparently agreed with him. He had lost the edgy restlessness that had seemed so much a part of him for so many years.

She had smiled and opened her mouth to greet him, forgetting for just an instant where things stood between them.

Before she could say anything, he looked straight through her, then turned around and walked out of the cafeteria, leaving his food behind, as if he'd just stumbled into a leper colony.

No, not quite right. David was a compassionate, caring physician. He would rush right in to help anyone who was ill, especially if they suffered from a potentially life-threatening condition.

Apparently, she ranked somewhere well below a colony of lepers in her older brother's estimation. He couldn't even manage to bring himself to say hello to her.

Anna sighed. She had to stop being so maudlin about her siblings. She had made her choice when she had suggested Walnut River General as a possible acquisition target to her superiors at NHC. She had created this situation and she had no business moping about it.

"Looks like you're up," someone said behind her and Anna realized with some chagrin that while she had been sitting brooding, the line had moved forward and she was next to checkout.

She jerked her tray forward along the metal rails then watched with horror as her diet soda toppled sideways from the jolt. In her distraction after the scene with David, she apparently hadn't fastened on the plastic lid securely. As the cup fell, the contents splashed out—directly on the woman standing behind her.

Anna's face burned and she wanted nothing more than to leave her tray there and just escape. Still, she forced herself to turn to the other woman and found an elegant, pretty redhead wearing a pale green Donna Karan suit and a white blouse that now sported a golfball-sized caramel-colored stain on the front.

The woman looked vaguely familiar but Anna was quite certain she had never met her.

"I am so sorry," Anna exclaimed. "I'll give you my card. Please send me the bill for the dry cleaning."

The woman's smile was remarkably gracious. "Don't worry about it. This was my least favorite blouse, anyway."

"I'm sure that's not true."

The woman laughed. "Well, maybe second least-favorite. I've got an orange thing in my closet that's really a disaster."

She narrowed her gaze, her smile slipping just a fraction. "You're Anna, aren't you?"

Anna's stomach clenched. She really wasn't sure she could handle another confrontation right now. The woman was liable to dump her entire lunch all over her.

"Yes," she said warily. "I'm sorry, have we met?"

"No, though I was at your father's funeral. And I've just seen a picture of you in Peter's office."

"You…you have?"

"It was a picture taken at your father's last birthday party and has all four of you together. I've been wanting to meet you for a long time. I'm Bethany Holloway."

Bethany Holloway? *This* was Peter's fiancée?

Here was another stark reminder of the rift between her and her siblings. Her brother was marrying this woman in a few weeks and this was the first time Anna had even met her.

"Your total is six dollars and twenty-three cents," the cashier said pointedly. "You can go ahead and get another soda if you want."

Anna realized abruptly that she was holding up an entire line of hungry people. "Let me at least pay for your lunch," she said to Bethany.

"You don't have to do that."

"I do," Anna insisted. The cashier gave her a new total. Anna handed her a twenty and pocketed the change.

"That was not necessary, but thank you, anyway," Bethany said, moving with her out of the way so others could pay for their lunches.

"You're welcome," Anna replied. "I mean it about the dry cleaning."

Bethany shook her head. "I've got on-the-go stain removal stuff in my office. Soda should come out in a flash. If nothing else, I always keep a spare shirt in my office and I can change into that one after lunch. Please don't worry about it."

Anna had to admit, she was astonished. Bethany Holloway was actually smiling at her. She couldn't quite figure out why. Not only had Anna dumped soda all over her, but Anna would have assumed Peter's fiancée would be firmly on the opposite side of the family divide.

"I was supposed to meet Peter for lunch but he had an emergency. I guess I need to get used to that if I'm marrying a doctor, right? I hate to eat alone, though—are you meeting someone for lunch?"

"Uh, no."

In truth, she had planned to take the tray up to the tiny little hole in the wall office J.D. had begrudged her to go over the accounts.

"Good," Bethany said. "We can sit together and you can tell me all of Peter's secrets."

Her warm friendliness left Anna feeling off kilter, as if one of her heels was two inches shorter than the other, and she didn't know quite how to respond.

"I'm afraid I don't know any. Of Peter's secrets, I mean. I've been away from Walnut River for a long time."

Bethany smiled. "That's all right, then. You can tell me all of your secrets."

Bethany headed for a table without looking to see if Anna followed or not. Anna again fought the urge to flee to the relative safety of her borrowed office.

But she wasn't a coward. For some strange reason, her brother's fiancée wanted to talk to her and Anna didn't see that she had much of a choice but to comply.

Chapter Five

Anna slid into the booth opposite Bethany, wondering how she was possibly going to be able to swallow with these nerves jumping around in her stomach.

It was silly, really.

She had no reason to be apprehensive around Peter's fiancée. By all appearances, Bethany was kind and gracious. Anna didn't know many women of her acquaintance who could handle having a soda slopped all over them with such aplomb—especially when the one doing the slopping was on the outs with her fiancé.

She tried to focus on what she knew about Bethany and remembered that at one point she had been in favor of the merger, identified by NHC as a definite vote for their side. She decided there was no reason to talk around the issue.

"I understand you're an efficiency expert here at the

hospital," she said when they were both settled. "And you've been on the governing board of directors for a little over a year."

Bethany raised a slim auburn eyebrow. "NHC has a good research team. I suppose you have complete dossiers on every board member."

Anna toyed with a piece of lettuce, refusing to feel like a corporate stoolie. "You know how it works. It pays to know the players. At one point you were considered firmly on our side."

"I was. Absolutely."

"But you've gone on record opposing it now," she said. "Is that because of Peter?"

It was a rude question and one she regretted as soon as the words came out. To her vast relief, Bethany only laughed.

"Oh, he would love to hear you say that. No, I didn't change my vote because of my relationship with your brother. From an efficiency standpoint, the merger still makes sense. I won't deny that."

She paused and appeared to be considering her words with delicate care. "From a human standpoint, though, I'm not convinced Northeastern HealthCare has the best interest of our patients at heart."

Just like that, Anna automatically slid back on the defensive. "If you look at the statistics, you'll find we have a great track record at other hospitals of improving patient access to care while saving money at the same time."

"I know all the arguments, Anna. I promise, I've read the reports on NHC. We could debate this endlessly and I'm not sure we would get anywhere. There are compelling arguments on both sides but right now I have to go with my gut, that this deal isn't right for Walnut River General at the moment."

She lifted a slim hand to forestall any further arguments. "Let's talk about something else, okay? I'm sure you get enough arguments from everyone and I'd really like us to be friends."

Anna wasn't sure that was possible, given the current situation, but she found she desperately liked the idea of having Bethany as a friend.

"I hate to be a bridezilla," Bethany continued, "but can we talk about my wedding?"

Anna gulped. She would almost rather stage a public debate on the merger right there in the cafeteria than talk about her brother's wedding. Short of getting up and leaving her food there at the table in her rush to escape, she wasn't sure how to wiggle out of it.

"Okay," she said slowly.

"You're coming, aren't you?" Bethany asked. "Last I checked you hadn't sent an RSVP. You did receive the invitation, right? I sent it to your New York apartment and was hoping it didn't miss you on your way here."

Yes, she had received it. She had pulled out the elegant sheet of calligraphied vellum and had stared at it for a long time, sorrow aching through her at the distance between her and her siblings.

In the end, she had slipped the invitation into her briefcase, though she had absolutely no intention of accepting.

"Yes. I got it," she admitted.

"And? You're coming, aren't you?"

"Does Peter know you sent me an invitation?"

Bethany blinked but not before Anna was certain she

saw a little glimmer of uncertainty in the depths of her green eyes.

"Of course," she answered, but somehow Anna was certain she wasn't telling the whole truth.

The vague suspicion, that tiny hesitation on Bethany's part, was enough to remove any lingering doubt in her mind about whether to attend the wedding.

"I'm really happy for you and Peter," Anna said. "But...I don't think I can make it."

"Why not?" Bethany asked bluntly.

The other woman might look as soft and fragile as puff pastry but that impression was obviously an illusion. She was glad for it, Anna thought. Bethany Holloway appeared more than a match for her oldest brother, who could sometimes be domineering and set in his ways.

"The last thing you need on your wedding day is to have a simmering family feud boil over and explode all over the place. It would be better if I stayed away."

"Oh, don't be ridiculous!"

If Bethany hadn't sounded so sincere, Anna might have taken offense. Instead she merely shook her head.

"It's not ridiculous. None of them are even talking to me right now. I ran into David ten minutes ago just outside and he looked right through me as if I wasn't even there. I got the same treatment from Ella last week when I bumped into her on the fourth floor."

Compassion flickered in the depths of Bethany's green eyes. "That must have hurt."

For half a second, she thought about shrugging off her sympathy but the sincere concern in Bethany's expression warmed somewhere cold and hollow inside her.

"Like crazy," she admitted quietly. "Ella used to be my best friend. Now she won't even talk to me."

"I'm so sorry."

"I knew they would be upset that I'd chosen to work for Northeastern HealthCare. I guess I'd hoped they would at least try to hear my side of things."

"You Wilders all feel passionately for the things you care about," Bethany said.

"I'm not one of them," Anna said quickly.

As far as she was concerned, that was the crux of the problem. She didn't have the Wilder medical gene and she didn't have their dogmatism.

"I'm sure Peter told you I was adopted," she said when Bethany just looked puzzled.

A strange, furtive look flickered in those green eyes. Bethany opened her mouth to respond then closed it again, as if she had suddenly reconsidered her words.

"I've heard the story," she finally said. "Peter told me he was ten years old when your father brought you home and claimed he found you on the steps of Walnut River General. It was a defining moment in his life."

She stared. "In Peter's life or my father's?"

"Well, I'm sure in your father's life as well. But I meant Peter."

"How?"

"As the oldest son he felt responsible for the rest of you, and for your mother's feelings, as well. I know she… wasn't well those few years before you came into the family."

A polite way of saying Alice Wilder had suffered deep depression and had ended up medicated in the years before Anna's adoption.

"Yes," she answered warily. Her relationship with

her mother had always been complicated. She had loved Alice, as every child loves her mother, but their relationship had always felt strained. Cumbersome. Deep in her heart, she had wondered why her mother didn't quite seem to love her as much as she did Peter, David and Ella.

James had more than compensated for any coolness from Alice but the pain still lingered.

"Your father worked a great deal," Bethany said. "As the oldest son, Peter always felt responsible for everyone's happiness. His mother's. David's. And then when you and Ella came along, for yours, as well. I don't know that that has changed much over the years. He loves you very much, Anna. And he misses you. They all do."

She might find it a little easier to believe if she hadn't experienced firsthand the compelling evidence that none of the Wilders was thrilled to have her back in town.

"He might be angry with you right now over the merger," Bethany continued, "but that's because he feels as if your father's legacy is threatened."

Anna's frustration erupted. "It's a hospital! It's walls and a roof and medical equipment! What kind of legacy is that? James's legacy ought to be the children he left behind. Children who have grown into four fairly decent adults who are doing their best to make the world a better place for others. That's a legacy to be proud of, not the hospital where he spent every waking moment he should have been spending with kids who needed their father!"

She was mortified the moment she heard the heat and lingering bitterness behind her own words.

She thought she had gotten over all that when she

walked away from medical school—the secret fear that her father would only love her if she became a doctor like he was, if she devoted all her energy to the hospital where he had rescued her.

How many times had she heard that story about finding her on the hospital steps? Too damn many.

You were the only infant ever left at Walnut River General. I knew the minute I saw you that you belonged in our family. James always used to say that with pride in his eyes—whether for the hospital he loved or for her, she was never quite sure.

She couldn't help wondering what might have happened to her if she had been left somewhere else besides the hospital—an orphanage, a garbage can, even James's and Alice's own doorstep.

Would he have wanted her at all?

"From what I've heard of your father, I know he was very proud of each of his children," Bethany said.

Each of the three physicians in the family, perhaps. As for her, Ella and their brothers wondered why she'd kept her job with NHC a secret for two years. She could just imagine what James's reaction would have been if he had known before his death that she had gone to work for a corporate entity he would have considered the enemy.

The shock alone would have brought on that fatal heart attack.

She forced a smile. "I'm sure you're right," she murmured, though the lie tasted like acid.

"Peter is your brother, despite your current… estrangement. He will feel your absence at the wedding deeply, no matter what he might say. Will you at least think about coming?"

Anna shook her head. "You're a very persistent bride, aren't you?"

Bethany smiled. "That's a polite way to say stubborn as a one-eyed mule, isn't it? I can be, when the situation demands it."

She might not be the woman Anna would have expected her brother to fall for, but she decided she very much liked Bethany Holloway. Somehow she had a feeling they *would* become good friends. It was a comforting thought.

"I'll think about it," she answered. "That's all I can promise right now. The wedding is still three weeks away. A great deal can happen in three weeks."

Bethany opened her mouth to respond, but before the words could escape, Anna's attention was drawn to a trio of men entering the cafeteria—J. D. Sumner, new chief of staff Owen Mayfield, and Richard Green.

Richard spotted her and Bethany at almost the exact same instant. She saw something bright and luminous flash in his eyes for just an instant before it faded.

A moment later, he excused himself from the other men and made his way toward their corner booth.

Anna was aware of several things simultaneously—the funny little dip and shiver of her stomach as he approached, the clean, elegant lines of his summer-weight charcoal suit that made him look as gorgeous as if he had just stepped out of a gentlemen's magazine, the faint lines of fatigue around his blue eyes.

Most of all, she was aware of how her heart seemed to tremble just at the sight of him.

"Good afternoon."

He smiled freely at Bethany, but his light expression faded when he turned his attention to Anna.

She tried to ignore the shaft of hurt piercing through her at the contrast, aware of how very tired she was becoming of fighting battles with everyone she encountered at Walnut River General.

"J.D. was just telling me you were working here this morning," Richard said.

"Yes. The hospital's legal counsel apparently won't give permission for me to take any records off site," she said pointedly.

"All in one more effort to make your life more difficult, I'm sure," Richard said dryly.

She made a face. "It certainly does. But the administration has been kind enough to give me a temporary work space. I suppose I should be grateful they stopped short of blocking access completely."

"Since the municipal council has approved your inquiries, legally there's nothing the hospital can do to stop you."

His hard voice stopped just shy of outright hostility but it was enough to make Bethany blink and Anna bristle.

"No. I don't suppose there is," she said evenly. "Short of tackling me in the parking lot and tying me to a bench somewhere."

Something warm and slightly naughty sparked in his eyes for just an instant, then it was gone. Still, her insides shivered in reaction.

"I was trying to reach Alfred Daly but perhaps you can give him a message for me."

She gazed at him warily, wondering just how many other people from her past would she alienate before NHC succeeded in its efforts to absorb Walnut River General into its family of hospitals.

"All right," she answered.

"Please let him know I will be representing the hospital for the foreseeable future. My partner is taking an indefinite leave of absence."

She thought of the attorney she had met only a few times since coming to Walnut River. He had seemed very nice, if somewhat distracted. Never once had he looked at her with anything resembling scorn, unlike others she could mention.

"Everything's all right, I hope?"

His expression registered surprise at her concern and he hesitated for just a moment before answering. "I'm sure it will be."

He said he was representing the hospital for the forseeable future, which must include the NHC merger negotiations. The jitters in her stomach became a sudden stampede. There was no escaping the grim realization that she would have no choice but to work closely with Richard Green if she wanted to pull off this merger.

"I will let him know," she answered coolly, pleased her voice didn't reveal any of her inner torment. "I should tell you in the interest of disclosure that your partner asked for copies of the reports I'm working on. Our legal team agreed to provide them as a show of good faith to demonstrate our willingness to cooperate as fully as possible. I can have them ready for you first thing in the morning."

He frowned. "No chance they'll be ready before then? I'm going to be in court the rest of the week. Tonight would be the best chance for me to find time to look at them."

She quickly considered her options.

She could be an obstructionist and tell him no, that she couldn't possibly finish the financial study until the next day. But that wasn't exactly true. She was close to being done and with a little accelerated effort, could have things wrapped up in a few hours.

"I can try to finish them tonight and run them over to you at home."

Again, the flicker of surprise in his expression frustrated her. Once they had been close friends. He had known her better than just about anyone in her life, except maybe Ella. Did he really have to register such astonishment when she tried to be cooperative and do something nice?

"That would be perfect. Thank you."

Still annoyed, she gave him a cool, polite smile. "You're welcome. Give me your address and I'll run them by when I'm done."

"You don't need an address. I'm living in my parents' house. It was too much upkeep for my mother so I bought it from her after my father died. She lives in a condo just a few blocks away."

Anna had always liked Diane Green. She had been warm and gracious, always willing to open her home to Richard's friends. His house had been the high-school hangout, with its huge game room and built-in swimming pool.

It would be a lovely place to raise a son, she thought.

"I don't know what time I'll be finished. It might be late."

"That's fine. I'll be up late prepping for court in the morning."

She nodded and managed to hang on to her polite smile when he said a cool goodbye to her and a much warmer one to Bethany before he returned to J.D. and Dr. Mayfield.

She watched his elegant frame walk away for just a moment longer than she should have. She knew it as soon as she turned back to Bethany and found Peter's fiancée watching her with upraised eyebrows.

"I'm sorry. What were we talking about?"

"My wedding." Bethany grinned suddenly. "But that's not important right now. I would much rather hear what's going on with you and sexy Richard Green."

"Going on? Absolutely nothing."

She cursed her fair skin as she felt heat soak her cheeks. She couldn't bluff her way out of a blasted paper bag, the way she turned red at the slightest provocation.

Bethany didn't look at all convinced. "Are you sure about that? There was enough energy buzzing between the two of you to light up the Las Vegas strip."

"We grew up together. His house is just a few blocks away from where we grew up and we were always good friends."

"And?"

She could feel her blush deepen as she remembered that last night together and the kisses and touches she had never been able to forget.

For one shining moment she had held paradise in her hands.

He had offered her everything she'd ever dreamed of. He had told her he was in love with her. She could still remember her giddy joy, how she had wanted nothing more than to hold on tight and never let go.

She had wanted so much to grab hold of what he was offering—but she hadn't been able to figure out a way to break free of her family's expectations while holding tight to Richard at the same time.

Seeing him again, learning more about the man he had become, made her see how immature a response that had been for a girl of twenty-two years.

She had been so certain she had to take all or nothing,

to sever all ties to Walnut River if she wanted to escape the immovable path her family expected her to take.

But Richard had never placed the kind of unrealistic expectations on her that her father had. He had even told her if medical school wasn't for her, she needed to decide earlier, rather than later.

What would have happened if she had decided she could still drop out of medical school and pursue her business career while maintaining a relationship with Richard?

It wasn't at all helpful to speculate on the hypothetical, she reminded herself harshly. The truth was, she had turned her back on Richard when she had turned her back on her family. That ship had sailed, and all that. She would never know, so there was absolutely nothing to be gained by speculating on what might have been.

"There's nothing between us," she assured Bethany. "I haven't seen him in eight years and now we're on opposite sides of the hospital merger."

Which might as well be a twenty-foot high fence topped with another five feet of razor wire for all the chance she had of breaching it.

Chapter Six

"Dad! You shut my door! You know I can't sleep with my door shut all the way!"

Ethan's voice echoed down the hall, drawing nearer with each word, and Richard sighed as he straightened and closed the oven door where he'd just set his dinner to warm.

Here we go, he thought.

He turned and, just as he expected, he found Ethan in the doorway wearing his Buzz Lightyear pajamas, his little mouth set in a disgruntled expression.

"Sorry, bud. I forgot."

"You forgot everything tonight! You forgot to give me an Eskimo kiss and during bathtime you didn't even ask me my five fun things."

Guilt pinched at him and he wished that he could split himself into two or three people to get everything in his life accomplished. His court appearance in the morning weighed heavily on his mind—but his son always had to come first.

"I'm sorry. It's been a long day," he said. "I'll do better tomorrow, okay? Come on, let's get you back into bed and you can tell me your five fun things."

"Okay."

It was a tradition they had started as soon as Ethan learned to talk, where each evening they would share five interesting things they had seen or done that day.

Ethan's list usually consisted of games or toys he and his nana had played with that day. It was sometimes a scramble but Richard usually tried for a little creativity in his own contributions to the game. Today he was afraid he was running on empty.

"You said that yesterday," Ethan exclaimed when Richard tried to use the colorful clown that stood outside the local hamburger joint with a signboard and a pleading expression as one of his five interesting things to report about his day.

"But this time he had on one of those crazy rainbow wigs," Richard said. "I didn't tell you that yesterday."

Much to his relief, his five-year-old accepted his logic and climbed into bed obediently.

They exchanged hugs and the obligatory Eskimo kisses then Richard tucked him in for the second time that evening. "This time I'm spraying glue on your pillow so you can't get out again."

While Ethan giggled he pretended to spray an aerosol can around his son's bed, his hair, behind his back. "There. Now you're stuck. You're not going anywhere."

"Okay. But don't forget to come unstick me in the

morning before you leave. Nana said we can go to the park after breakfast and I don't want to miss it."

He smiled and kissed his son on the nose. "I will. I've got magic un-stick spray just waiting for morning, I promise."

This time, he left Ethan's door slightly ajar and returned to the kitchen. His stomach rumbled at the delicious smells starting to emanate from the oven. A quick check of the timer on the oven revealed he still had twenty minutes before his mother's lasagna would be finished. That should be long enough to go over his opening argument one more time—that is, if he could hang on to his limited concentration long enough to do the job.

He sighed again, all too grimly aware of the reason he had been so distracted all evening.

One word.

Anna.

Since bumping into her at the hospital cafeteria earlier, he hadn't been able to shake her from his mind. The curve of her cheekbones, the little shell of her ear, the fragile vulnerability in the set of her mouth he wondered if anyone else could see.

She said she would drop off her report that night and he felt as if he had spent the entire evening in a state of suspended animation, just waiting for the doorbell to ring.

He knew damn well those feelings swirling through him were entirely inappropriate, but he couldn't seem to move beyond them.

He couldn't wait to see her again, foolish as he knew that was.

He had absolutely no sense when it came to Anna

Wilder. It was a rather depressing thing to acknowledge about himself.

Just how long did he have to carry a torch for her? If someone had asked him a week ago if he still had feelings for Anna, he would have busted up laughing at the very idea. He never even thought of her anymore, he would have answered quite smugly. How could he be foolish enough to think he still had feelings for the woman?

He thought he had done a pretty good job of purging her from his thoughts. Eight years was a long time to burn for a woman who had made it plain she didn't want him.

But now she was back in Walnut River and every single time he saw her, she seemed to become more and more entangled in his thoughts until he had a devil of a time thinking about anything else.

Did he still have feelings for her? He certainly wasn't about to admit something so dangerous, even to himself. Sure, he was still attracted to her. He certainly couldn't deny that, especially since he wasn't able to stop himself looking at his watch every five seconds and had even gone out once to check that the doorbell was working right.

He needed to get out more. He could count on one hand the number of dates he'd had in the years since his marriage imploded.

Richard sighed, wishing again for a clone or two. When, exactly, was he supposed to find time for a social life? Between working to establish his practice and trying to be the best father possible to Ethan, his time was fragmented enough.

What if Anna hadn't blown him off eight years ago and left town? If she weren't here representing NHC? If they didn't have diametrically opposing goals regarding Walnut River General Hospital?

What was the point in wasting time with useless hypotheticals? Richard chided himself. He had too damn much to do tonight to indulge in fantasies of what might have been.

The fact was, she *had* walked away, she *did* work for NHC and he would need to keep all his wits about him to keep her and her corporation from taking over the hospital he cared about.

He would do well to remember all those things, Richard thought as he forced himself to turn back to his laptop, angled on a corner of the kitchen table where he had been working earlier while Ethan played with trucks on the floor.

The screen had just come out of sleep mode when he heard a car engine out front. The swirl of anticipation he'd tried so hard to tamp down became a wild cyclone. So much for the little pregame lecture, he thought ruefully.

A click of the keyboard sent the monitor back to sleep, then he hurried to the front door. He reached it just an instant after she rang the doorbell.

"Oh!" she exclaimed when he opened the door, her hand still half raised to the bell. "Hello."

"Sorry to startle you. I was trying to catch you before you rang the doorbell so you didn't wake Ethan. I have a tough time getting him back down to sleep if something disturbs him."

"I'm so sorry. I didn't even think. I should have knocked."

"No. It's fine. I doubt he's even asleep yet."

The words had barely escaped his mouth when Ethan popped his head out of his bedroom, his hair tousled but his eyes not at all sleepy. They lit up with excitement when he saw Anna.

"Hi!" he exclaimed brightly. "I heard the doorbell but I didn't know it was you."

"Hi, Ethan!"

Richard tried to steel his emotions against the soft delight in her eyes as she looked at his son.

"I thought you were glued to the bed," he said dryly to his son.

Ethan giggled. "I guess the glue must have worn off. When I heard the doorbell, I was able to climb right out. I don't know how."

"What a surprise," he muttered.

Anna sent him a sideways, laughing look that stole his breath.

"Anna, can you read me one more story?" Ethan wheedled. "If you do, I promise, I'll stay in my bed this time for good."

"I guess that's up to your father."

"Daddy, can she?"

He didn't want her to feel obligated, but if the antici-pation on her features was any indication, she was excited at the prospect.

"All right. Just one story, and then to bed this time to stay. You have to pinky swear."

Ethan had to hold down his other four fingers with his left hand in order to extend the little finger on his right, but his features were solemn and determined as he inter-locked with Richard's pinky.

"I swear. I won't get out again, Daddy, if Anna can read me one story. Oh, and if she can give me one more Eskimo kiss, too."

"Deal," she said quickly, before Richard could even think about negotiating different terms.

She reached for Ethan's hand and the two of them headed for his son's bedroom. Richard followed, unable to resist leaning against the door jamb and watching as they carefully selected the right story.

He wasn't sure what he felt as he watched Anna slip off her heels and sit on the edge of Ethan's bed. His son cuddled up to her as if they were best friends and after a moment, she slipped her arm around him, their blond heads close together.

She read the story, about a worm keeping a diary about his life, with pathos and humor. When she turned the last page, Ethan sighed with satisfaction.

"I sure do wish I could have another one. You're a really good story reader."

"You made a pinky swear, remember," Anna said with a smile. She slipped her shoes back on then leaned in and rubbed her nose against his.

"You smell good," Ethan declared, and Richard wondered how his son had possibly become such a lady killer with the lousy example he had for a father in that department.

Anna laughed. "So do you. Now go to sleep, okay?"

Ethan snuggled down into the covers, his eyelids beginning to droop. "Okay. Will you come to another one of my baseball games? I only have two more."

She glanced at Richard, then back at his son. "Sure," she answered. "I'd love to."

"You have to promise or else I can't go to sleep."

She laughed again. "You're a born negotiator, Ethan, my man."

"What's a go-she-a-tor?"

"Negotiator. It means somebody who works out deals with people. You agree to do something as long as I do something else in return."

"I just want you to come to my baseball game."

"I said I would."

"Is that a promise?"

She shook her head. "All right! I promise."

He grinned with satisfaction. "Thank you for the story, Anna."

"You're very welcome, sir."

"Will you come back and read to me again sometime?"

She paused for just an instant and Richard thought he saw a faint brush of color on her cheeks before she tugged Ethan's covers up to his chin. "We'll have to see about that one. Good night."

"Good night," Richard added. "This time I mean it."

"Okay. 'Night, Dad."

He closed the door behind Anna—remembering just in time to leave it slightly ajar.

"I'm sorry you had to do that."

"I'm not." She smiled softly. "He's darling."

"He's a manipulative scoundrel who's going to end up behind bars someday."

"It's a good thing his father is a lawyer, then."

And his mother, Richard thought. The blunt reminder of Lynne and all the mistakes he had made was like jumping into a mountain stream in January.

Anna picked up her briefcase and rifled through it for a moment, pulling out a slim maroon folder.

"Here's the report I promised you. I'm sorry I didn't get it here earlier. I meant to have it done two hours ago but I, uh, had a bit of a tough time getting some of the information I needed."

Translation: Those who opposed the NHC takeover were making life as difficult as possible for Anna. He didn't need her to spell it out for him when he could see the exhaustion in her eyes and the set of her mouth.

A twinge of pity flickered through him. None of this could be easy for her.

"Have you had dinner?" he asked. The moment the words were out, he regretted them but it was too late to yank them back.

She stared. "Dinner?"

"You know, that meal you traditionally eat at the end of the day?"

"Oh, that one." She smiled. "I guess my answer would have to be no, not yet. That's next on my agenda."

"I've got some of my mom's lasagna in the oven. You're welcome to join me."

Surprise flickered over those lovely features. "It does smell delicious. But I've got Lilli out in the car. Since my place is on the way here, I stopped on the way to check on her and she begged me to bring her along."

He should let her use the excuse as a way to avoid the meal but he found himself reluctant to give up that easily. "She's welcome to come inside while we eat. I don't mind."

"Are you sure? I wouldn't want to provide Ethan more ammunition in the Great Puppy War."

"He'll never know. Besides, maybe having Lilli underfoot during dinner, begging for scraps, will shore up my sagging resolve to wait a few more years before we enter pethood."

She raised an eyebrow. "Excuse me, but my dog is extremely well-behaved. She never begs. She just asks nicely."

Anna was so beautiful when she smiled, he thought, and cursed himself all over again for the impulse to invite her to stay—an impulse, he admitted, that had probably been simmering inside him all evening. Why else would he have thrown an entire lasagna in the oven instead of just grabbing a TV dinner?

He had absolutely no willpower around Anna Wilder and no common sense, either. He had a million things to do before court in the morning. He certainly didn't have time to spend the evening entertaining a woman he had vowed to keep at a distance.

Despite the knowledge, he found he couldn't quite bring himself to regret extending the invitation.

Not yet, anyway.

He wanted her to have dinner with him? Anna wouldn't have been more surprised if Richard had met her at the door doing the hula in a muumuu and lei.

A wise woman would tell him to forget it and get the heck out of there. She had very few defenses left against Richard Green and his adorable son, and she was very much afraid she was in danger of falling hard for him all over again.

"Go and get Lilli and by the time you come back in, the lasagna will be on the table."

She paused for only half a second before surrendering. How could she do anything else, when this was the most amiable and approachable she'd seen Richard since coming back to Walnut River?

"All right," she said. "I'll admit, my mouth has been watering since I walked in the door."

And not just because of the delectable smells of lasagna wafting from the kitchen, she was forced to admit to herself. Richard Green in his charcoal business suit was gorgeous, in a dangerous, formidable kind of way. Richard Green in his stocking feet, faded Levi's and a casual cotton shirt with the sleeves rolled up was completely irresistible.

She quickly collected Lilli from her car and juggled the excited dog and her umbrella as she hurried back up the walkway to his house. He stood in the open doorway waiting for her and her stomach gave a funny little tremble at the sight of him.

"Behave yourself," she ordered as she set Lilli down on the tile of the entryway, the stern reminder intended for her own benefit as much as her dog's.

"I'll do my best," Richard answered dryly. He reached for her umbrella and Anna slipped off her heels, lining them neatly by the door.

Lilli's tail wagged like crazy as she trotted around the house, sniffing in corners and under furniture. With the excuse of keeping a close eye on her inquisitive little dog, Anna managed to assuage her own curiosity about Richard's house.

Their group of friends had spent many hours at his place through high school. With the built-in swimming pool and the huge media and game room in the basement, it was a natural teen hangout. She remembered pool parties and study sessions and movie nights.

Seeing it now after years away was rather disconcerting. Little was as she remembered.

"Your house has changed."

He smiled. "Just a bit. When I bought the place after

my dad died, I had the interior completely redone. New paint, new carpet, took out a wall here or there to open it up. The house had great bones but everything was a little outdated."

"Diane didn't mind?"

"Are you kidding? My mother loved helping oversee the redecorating, as long as it was my own dime."

"It looks great," she assured him as Lilli investigated a cluster of houseplants climbing a matte black ladder in the corner.

The house was elegant but comfortable, with solid furniture that looked as if it would stand up well to a busy five-year-old.

"I'm just going to throw together a salad," Richard said. Do you want to come back to the kitchen?"

"Sure."

With Lilli close on their heels, she followed him down the hall. Here were the most dramatic renovations she had seen in the house. She remembered the kitchen as a rather small, cramped space with dark wood cupboards and a long breakfast bar that took up most of the space.

This must be where he had talked about knocking down walls because it was about twice the size as she remembered. Rain clicked against skylights overhead and in place of the breakfast bar, a huge island with a sink and second stovetop dominated the space.

The colors reminded her of a Tuscan farmhouse, warm red brick floors, mustard yellow walls with white accents. It was a dream of a kitchen, airy and welcoming and vastly different from the tiny sliver of a kitchen in her apartment in Chelsea.

"Would you like a glass of wine?"

"Yes, please," she decided, perching on one of the stools at the island.

He seemed very much at home in his own kitchen and she knew darn well she shouldn't find that so sexy.

She sipped her wine and watched him work while Lilli sniffed the corners of the kitchen. The silence between them was surprisingly comfortable, like slipping into a favorite jacket in the autumn.

"So who was giving you a tough time today?" Richard asked after a moment.

She flashed him a quick look. "How do you know somebody was?"

"You never turned an assignment in late in your life when we were in school. If I remember correctly, you always turned everything in at least a day or two early. I figured the only reason you would be late with anything must have more to do with external forces."

"Clever as always, counselor."

"So who was it?"

She sighed, some of her peace dissipating at the reminder of the hurdles in front of her and their clear demarcation on opposite sides of the NHC front. "No one. Not really. I just had a...difficult time getting some of the information I needed. I don't blame anyone. I completely understand there are mixed feelings at the hospital about the merger."

His laugh was dry. "Mixed feelings is one way to put it."

"Believe it or not, I do understand why not everyone likes the idea of an outside company coming in and messing with the status quo. I understand about tradition and continuity and about safety in the familiar. But I wish people could approach this with an open mind. If people would look beyond their preconceptions, perhaps they might see how Northeastern HealthCare is looking at innovative changes that would benefit both the hospital and the community in general...."

She caught herself just before launching into a passionate argument once more. "I'm sorry. I really don't want to talk about the hospital tonight. After living and breathing this merger from the moment I awoke this morning, I could use a break. Do you mind?"

He stopped mixing the salad, watching her with an unreadable expression for a moment before he suddenly offered a smile she felt clear down to her toes.

"Excellent idea. I wouldn't want to ruin by mother's delicious lasagna by launching into a cross-examination."

He grabbed the salad and carried it through an arched doorway to the dining room.

Out of old habit, she grabbed plates from the cupboard where they had always been stored, finding an odd comfort that they were still there.

The silverware was also still in its familiar spot and she grabbed two settings and carried the utensils into the dining room.

Richard raised an eyebrow but said nothing as she helped him set the table. A moment later, he carried in the lasagna and placed it on the table then took a seat across from her.

Lilli stopped her wandering and curled up, her body a small warm weight on Anna's feet. The next few moments were busy with filling plates and topping wineglasses.

"If we're not going to talk about the hospital, what's a safe topic of conversation, then?" she asked when they were settled. "Baseball? The weather?"

"Who says it has to be safe?" The strangely intent look

in his eyes sent a shiver ripping down her spine. A strange undercurrent tugged and pulled between them.

"All right. Something dangerous, then. Your marriage?"

He gave a short laugh as he added dressing to his salad. "Not what I had in mind, but okay. What would you like to know?"

She had a million questions but one seemed paramount, even though she hardly dared ask it. "What happened?"

He shrugged, his expression pensive. "The grim truth is that it was a mistake from start to finish. I met Lynne at Harvard. She was brilliant, ambitious. Beautiful. In our last year, we started seeing each other, mostly just for fun. Nothing serious. In fact, we both planned to go our separate ways after graduation."

"But?"

He sighed, sudden shadows in his eyes. "A few weeks before we were to take the bar exam, she found out she was pregnant."

She tried to picture a younger version of Richard as she remembered him, perhaps with a few less laugh lines around the corners of his eyes. The Richard she knew always took his responsibilities seriously. She wasn't at all surprised that he would step up to take care of the child he fathered, only that he and Ethan's mother would make things official.

"Marriage is a huge leap of faith for two people who were set to go their separate ways, even with a child on the way."

"I think we both badly wanted to believe we could make it work. On paper, it seemed a good solution. We were both attorneys, we had shared interests, we enjoyed each other's company. I think we both tried to convince ourselves we were in love and could make it work. But

Lynne wasn't ready for a family. She tried, but I could see what a struggle it was for her. She…wasn't really cut out for motherhood. When Ethan was four months old, she received an unbeatable job offer overseas. Her dream position as lead counsel for an international shipping conglomerate. We both decided there was no good reason for her not to take it."

She heard the casual tone he tried to take but she also picked up the subtle sense of failure threading through his words.

He had always been competitive—captain of the debate team, a star on the baseball diamond, school valedictorian. He hated losing at anything and she imagined this particular failure would have hit him hard, especially with the loving example he had of marriage from his own parents.

The urge to touch him, to offer some small degree of comfort, was almost overwhelming. But they didn't have that kind of relationship, not anymore, so she curled one hand in her lap and picked up her wineglass with the other.

"I'm sorry," she murmured. "That couldn't have been an easy situation for you."

"We've done okay. My mother has been a lifesaver. I would have been lost without her."

They were quiet for a moment, the only sound Lilli's soft huffs and the rain clicking against the skylights.

"What about you?" he asked after a moment. "Any relationship mistakes in your past?"

Besides leaving you? The thought whispered through her mind unbidden and she had to shift her gaze away from his so he wouldn't read the truth in her eyes.

"Not really. Nothing serious, anyway."

"Why not?" Richard asked.

She decided to keep quiet about the fact that she hadn't had enthusiasm for dating in a long time, if ever. She had been too focused on her work, in making a success of herself—okay, in proving to her family that she could have a successful life outside medicine.

"I don't know. It hasn't really been a priority for me, I guess."

"I suppose it's a little tough having a long-term relationship when you travel so much."

"Something like that."

She really didn't want to discuss her love life—or decided absence of such a thing—with Richard Green.

"Okay, I just came up with the first dangerous topic of conversation. It's your turn."

"I thought I just asked you about the men you've dated. That's not dangerous enough for you?"

"Not at all. Trust me. The men I date are usually a boring lot. Accountants. Stockbrokers. Mild-mannered, one and all."

Not like you, she thought. Richard radiated a raw masculinity, even during a casual dinner at his home with his five-year-old sleeping only a few dozen feet away.

He studied her for a moment, and she had the vague impression of a lean and hungry wolf moving in for the kill.

"All right. You want dangerous? Why don't we talk about why you broke my heart eight years ago?"

Chapter Seven

Anna stared at Richard across the table, his mother's delicious lasagna congealing into a hard, miserable lump in her stomach.

The noises of the kitchen seemed unnaturally loud in the sudden tense silence, the whir of the refrigerator compressor sounding like a jet airplane taking off.

She wanted to scoop up her dog and race away from the awkwardness of his question and the guilty memories she couldn't escape.

"I didn't break your heart," she mumbled.

He lifted his wineglass in a mocking salute. "Excuse me, but I think I'm a little better judge of that than you are. You haven't seen me or my heart in eight years."

Though his words were light, she saw the barest hint of shadow in his eyes. She thought of all her reasons for leaving. What seemed so compelling eight years ago now seemed like a coward's way out.

"You couldn't have been too heartbroken," she pointed out. "You were married a few years later."

She didn't want to remember how she had holed up in her tiny shared apartment in New York City and wept for an entire day when Ella had called her with the news.

He was quiet for a moment and then he sent her a quizzical look. "Would you like to see a picture of Lynne?"

His question threw her off stride, especially in the context of their discussion. Why would he possibly think she would want to see a picture of his ex-wife right now?

She shrugged, not quite sure how to answer, and he slid away from the table and moved to a mantel in the great room off the kitchen. Through the doorway, she saw him take a picture from a collection on the mantel and a moment later he returned and held it out for her.

A younger, chubbier version of Ethan's winsome face filled most of the frame but just in the background, she could see a stunning woman with blond hair and delicate features. She looked at her son with love, certainly, but also a kind of baffled impatience.

"She's very beautiful."

"You don't see the resemblance?"

"I can't really tell. Ethan certainly has her eyes."

"You don't think she looks at all like you?"

Shocked to the core, she stared at the woman again. Is that the way he saw her? Cool and lovely and...distant?

"Her hair and her eye color, maybe," she protested. "That's all."

"You're absolutely right. That's where the resemblance ends. She's not you. Not at all. But here's the funny part.

I asked her out for the first time because she looked a bit like you. Since I couldn't have the real deal, I tried to convince myself an imitation was just as good. It was an idiotic mindset, one I'm ashamed I even entertained for a minute, but what can I say? I had been abruptly dumped by the only woman I ever loved."

Anna froze, reeling as if she'd just been punched in the stomach.

"Richard—"

"I didn't mean to say that. Withdrawn."

She had no idea what to say, to think. He had said that night he was falling in love with her but she had always attributed it to the heat of their passion.

After a long, awkward moment, he gave a rough laugh. "Dangerous is one thing when it comes to topics of conversation. Excruciatingly embarrassing is quite another."

She had to say something. She knew she did, especially after he stood up and returned his plate of half-eaten lasagna to the kitchen.

She rose, shaky inside. Lilli scampered ahead of her into the kitchen.

"I convinced myself it wasn't real," she finally said quietly when she joined him there. "What we shared that night. It was magical and beautiful and…miraculous. But I tried to tell myself we were just carried away by the night and…everything. You were my friend. Maybe my best friend. I couldn't let myself think of you in any other way or I wouldn't have been able to…to do what I knew I had to."

"Leave medical school and basically cut things off completely with your family."

"Yes," she admitted. "I loved my family. You know

that. But you also know what things were like for me with them. In my father's mind, there was no other possible career for any of his children. He refused to see how I was struggling that first year. How much I hated it. I tried to talk to him—all summer I tried! His advice was only to stick it out, that the second year would be better. *Wilders aren't quitters.* I can remember him telling me that as clearly as if he were sitting right here with us."

"He wanted you to follow in his footsteps."

"That's what *he* wanted. Not what *I* wanted. I was suffocating in med school. I hated it. The blood, the gore. The unending stress. Especially knowing I couldn't help everyone."

She could clearly remember the first time a patient whose care she had been observing had died. It had been a woman in her late fifties with end-stage breast cancer. She could remember the dispassionate attitude of the attending and the residents, in sharp contrast to the vast, overwhelming grief of the woman's husband and teenage daughters.

She had left the hospital that day feeling ill, heavy and ponderous, as if she carried the weight of that grief and the responsibility for their pain. Ridiculous, since she was only a first-year med student who hadn't even really been involved in the woman's care, but she hadn't been able to shake her guilt and the cries of the survivors that haunted her dreams.

"I knew if I made it through the second year, I would be trapped. I had to go, Richard. I didn't see any other choice."

He shrugged. "You could have stayed and stood up for yourself, fought for what you cared about."

Including him, she thought. She should have stayed and fought for what they could have shared.

"I missed you like crazy those first few months in the city," she confessed. "I think I missed you even more than I missed my family."

He leaned against the kitchen counter. "Forgive me if I find that a little hard to believe. At any point that year you could have picked up the phone or sent off an e-mail. But you cut me off completely. What the hell was I supposed to think? I just figured I was crazy and had imagined everything that happened that night."

"You didn't," she whispered, more miserable than she had been those first early days after she left.

"It doesn't matter now. Eight years ought to be long enough to get over a broken heart, don't you think?"

Something shifted between them, a subtle tug of awareness. "Yes," she managed.

"I thought I had done a pretty good job of putting you out of my head. Of course, then you had to ruin everything by coming back and making me remember."

"I'm sorry," she murmured.

His long exhalation stirred the air. "So am I."

Before she realized what he intended, he stepped forward and pulled her into his arms.

She caught her breath, unable to focus on anything but the blazing heat in his eyes as his mouth descended on hers.

The kiss was raw and demanding and she tasted eight years of frustration in it. Despite the undertone, everything inside her seemed to sigh in welcome.

Oh, she had missed this. Missed *him*. No other man had made her blood sing through her veins like Richard.

She knew she shouldn't return his kiss. If she were smart, she would jerk away right now and leave this house that contained so many memories for her.

She couldn't do it, though, not with this heat and wonder fluttering through her.

Her hands were trapped between their bodies and she could feel his heart pound beneath the cotton of his shirt, rapid and strong.

She spread her hands out, marveling at the taut muscles under her fingers. He might be an attorney but Richard still had the lithe athleticism of the baseball player he had been in high school.

His mouth deepened the kiss and she leaned into him, lost to everything but this moment, this man.

She wanted him. Just as she had eight years ago, she wanted him with a wild hunger that stole her breath.

He was the first one to pull away, wrenching his mouth free of hers and stepping away with such abruptness that she could only stare into the blue of his eyes, turned dark by desire.

He studied her for a long moment while she tried to catch her breath and catch hold of her wildly careening thoughts.

"Aren't you going to say anything?" he asked after a moment.

She might, if she could manage to string more than two words together in a brain that suddenly seemed disjointed and chaotic.

"That was…unexpected."

He lifted an eyebrow. "Was it?"

"Richard, I…"

He shook his head with a rough-sounding laugh. "Don't. Just don't. I was trying to remember what you tasted like. My curiosity has been appeased so let's just leave it at that."

That's all it had been? Curiosity? Not the kind of stunned desire that still churned through her body?

"Look, it's late. I'm due in court early tomorrow."

She drew in a shaky breath, mortified at her wild reaction to what had been purely experimentation on his part. "You're absolutely right. I never meant to stay so long."

If she had left fifteen minutes ago, none of this would have happened. She wouldn't have the taste of him on her lips or the scent of him, masculine and sexy, on her skin or the memory of his kiss burned into her brain.

She scooped up Lilli, absurdly grateful for the comfort of the dog's tiny, warm weight in her arms. He walked her to the door and helped her into her jacket, careful not to touch her more than completely necessary. He then held her umbrella while she slipped on her shoes.

"Thank you for dinner," she finally said.

"You're welcome," he answered, as formally as if they were two strangers meeting for coffee instead of lifelong friends who had just shared a moment of stunning passion.

She should say something more, but for the life of her, nothing else came to mind. "Good night, then."

He held the door open for her and she walked out into the night. She didn't bother with her umbrella, hoping the rain might cool her feverish skin and douse the regret that burned through her like a wind-whipped wildfire.

Richard stood at the window of his house watching her taillights gleam on the wet street before they disappeared.

So much for his intention to remain cool and composed around her. He had been about as calm as a blasted typhoon.

What had he been thinking to kiss her? It had been a mistake of epic proportion. Catastrophic.

He should have known he would skate so close to

losing his control. She'd always had that effect on him. What was it about Anna that revved his engine like that?

She was beautiful, yes, with that shimmery blond hair and those luscious blue eyes and skin that begged for his touch....

He jerked his mind away from all of Anna's many attractions. Beautiful as she might be, he had been around lovely women before, but Anna was the only one who ever tempted him to forget every ounce of common sense.

A few more moments of their embrace and he didn't know if he would have been able to stop—and that was with his son sleeping only a few rooms away.

She could break his heart again, if he let her.

Richard sighed. He wasn't about to let her. Not this time. He had learned his lesson well. Anna Wilde wasn't a woman he could count on. She had made that plain eight years ago. His foolishness over her had led him to some fairly disastrous mistakes.

He couldn't afford to lose his head over Anna again—not only for his own sake but for Ethan's.

He couldn't forget his son in this whole situation. Ethan had suffered enough from Richard's poor choices. If Richard had kept his wits around him, he would have known what a disaster his marriage to Lynne would be, that his choices would leave his son without a mother.

Richard's own mother did her best but she was now in her sixties and didn't have all the energy needed to keep up with a busy five-year-old boy.

For Ethan's sake, Richard couldn't afford to risk an involvement with a woman who already had a track record for leaving the things she cared about in pursuit of her career.

Hadn't that been exactly what Lynne had done? She

had tried the whole family and motherhood route but had fled when the responsibility had become too constricting.

Richard just had to use his head when it came to Anna Wilder. He was fiercely attracted to her and apparently that had only intensified over the years, so the only smart course would be to minimize contact with her as much as possible.

He couldn't avoid her completely. The NHC negotiations made that impossible, but he had to do everything he could to make sure their interactions in the future were formal and businesslike and as brief as he could manage.

It was the only way he would get through her temporary stay in Walnut River without hurting himself again.

The resolve managed to last more than a week.

Though he never lost focus of the hospital's fight for autonomy, other clients' legal issues took precedence for the next several days. He was busy, first with a trial date then with several evidentiary hearings.

He might not have seen Anna during that time, but unfortunately she was never far from his thoughts.

At random moments he found himself remembering the silky softness of her hair or the way her mouth trembled when he kissed her or her hands smoothing against his chest, burning through the fabric of his shirt.

He blew out a breath on his way to an appointment with J.D. to discuss strategy for the final board of directors' vote coming up in less than a week.

He supposed he shouldn't have been surprised when he walked into J.D.'s office to find Anna sitting in one of the office chairs, but the sight of her still stopped him in his tracks and he fiercely wished he could just turn around and head back out of the hospital.

She looked prim and proper again in a black jacket and skirt and he was furious at himself for the instant heat that jumped in his stomach.

Her eyes flashed to his and he saw an edge of discomfort, but not surprise. She must have had a little advance warning that he would be joining them.

Lucky her.

J.D. rose from his desk and shook his hand. "Hi, Richard. When I told Anna I was meeting with you this morning, she decided to steal a few minutes of our time so she could ask a couple of questions about our vendor accounting practices, since I told her I couldn't respond without legal counsel present."

J.D. met his gaze with a meaningful look and despite his unease, Richard had to hide a smile. Just the afternoon before, he had lectured the administrator about that very point—to avoid giving any information to NHC they weren't legally obligated to provide under the conditions the municipal council had set forth.

There were three chairs across from J.D.'s desk. As Anna sat in the middle chair, Richard had no choice but to sit beside her, where he was unable to escape her scent, fresh and lovely and sensual, or the heat shimmering off her skin.

"Anna, you're the one with the questions," J.D. said. "Where would you like to start?"

She opened her mouth, but before she could speak, Richard heard voices in the outer office through the open door.

"Hey, Tina," he heard someone greet J.D.'s assistant. "I just need to drop off some paperwork. I won't disturb him for long."

Richard recognized the voice and saw by the way

Anna's features paled that she did as well. A moment later, her oldest brother stuck his head in the doorway.

Dr. Peter Wilder always commanded attention wherever he went, with his dark hair and eyes, handsome features and the undeniable air of authority that seemed to emanate from him. He was very much like his father in that respect.

His gaze sharpened to a laser point when he saw his sister and the room suddenly buzzed with tension.

Richard wondered if Peter had seen the love that leapt into Anna's blue eyes when she had first seen him, before she quickly veiled her expression into cool indifference.

"Sorry. I didn't mean to interrupt."

J.D. rose from his desk and gestured to the vacant chair. "No, it's all right. We were just getting started. Why don't you join us? Anna had some questions about our patient accounting. As the former chief of staff, you might have some insight into that."

Peter looked as if he would rather shove a scalpel down his throat, but after a long, painfully awkward moment, he complied.

"You know I'm always happy to share my insight with NHC. Anything I can do to help," he drawled, and Anna's mouth tightened at his sarcasm.

"And NHC certainly appreciates your cooperation, Peter," she replied sweetly.

J.D. moved to referee before Peter could voice the heated response brewing in his dark eyes.

"So what are your questions?" he asked, interjecting.

She sent another swift look at her brother then seemed to stiffen her shoulders, becoming brisk and focused.

"My analysis of your records shows an unusually high

percentage of patient accounts the hospital deems uncollectible compared to hospitals of similar size and community demographics. Can you explain a reason why that might be the case?"

"I can." Peter broke in before J.D. could answer—or before Richard could vet either man's response.

"We're a local hospital that cares about the community. We refuse to turn anyone away and don't give a damn whether our patients are in the highest tax bracket or not. Our mission is to save lives, not bilk people out of their life savings."

"But according to my analysis, the hospital is losing a hundred thousand dollars a month and most of that is in uncollectible patient accounts," she pointed out. "How long do you think the taxpayers can continue to cover those losses?"

"Some of us care more about our patients' health than going after their wallets," he snapped.

"A noble sentiment, Peter. Exactly what I would have expected you to say. Just what Dad would have said."

Peter bristled. "What's that supposed to mean?"

She sighed and seemed to have forgotten both J.D. and Richard were there. "Nothing. It's all well and good to ride that high horse about focusing on patient care and battling back the evils of HMOs like some kind of league of superheroes with stethoscopes. But what's the alternative, Peter? For the hospital to just keep going deeper and deeper in the hole? Budgets are tightening everywhere. The city council has to do something. What if they decide to close the hospital instead of continuing to try in vain to plug the endless revenue drain?"

"So what you're saying is our patients are screwed either way. Better to get substandard care than none at all."

Anna's blue eyes flared. "NHC is not about substandard care! That's a simplistic argument. Our ultimate goal for all our member hospitals is to find more efficient, cost-effective ways to provide the same level of patient care."

"You really buy that company line? I thought you were supposed to be some hotshot business genius. I would have thought you were smarter than that."

Anna paled a shade lighter and J.D. moved to intervene but she cut him off. "Why can't you at least try to look at what NHC has to offer the hospital with a little rational objectivity?"

"I know what NHC is offering," her brother bit out. "Cut-rate services, increased patient load on physicians. Every day they play money games with people's health care, with their very lives! I can't believe you would pander to these bastards, Anna! What happened to your sense of decency?"

"You're as sanctimonious as ever. There's absolutely no reasoning with you. Yet another way you're just like Dad!"

"Leave him out of this! What do you think Dad would say if he knew you were doing this? Working for the enemy? Doing everything you can to destroy his legacy?"

Her mouth trembled just a bit before she firmly straightened it. While he had to admit he agreed with Peter, Richard still had to fight the urge to comfort her. A hand on her arm, a touch on her shoulder, whatever might ease the pain he couldn't believe her brother missed.

"I'm sure Dad would probably say the same thing you and David and Ella are saying about me. I'm a disgrace to the Wilder name. Isn't that what you all think?"

"Right now, hell, yes," Peter said. "You've always had

a chip on your shoulder but I never dreamed you'd take it this far, by trying to destroy something this family built nearly singlehandedly."

"Why don't we get back to your question." J.D. finally stepped in—about five minutes too late in Richard's opinion—but Anna ignored him.

"I imagine it's a huge comfort to you all that I'm not really a Wilder, then."

Peter's expression changed instantly and something very much like guilt flickered in his eyes.

"You are," he muttered.

"I'm not, Peter. We both know it."

J.D. cleared his throat. "Can you show us the figures that concern you in your report?"

She seemed to drag herself back to the meeting and Richard saw color soak her pale cheeks as she must have realized the detour the conversation had taken.

She took a deep breath and turned back to gaze blankly at the pages in front of her for a moment before she collected herself and rose. "I...yes." She looked flustered and Richard again fought the urge to rest a comforting hand on her arm.

"You'll see I've highlighted several pages in section eight of my report. I would appreciate if you and your legal counsel would formulate a response and get back to me."

"We can discuss it now. Richard's here to make sure I don't speak out of turn."

She twisted her mouth into a facsimile of a smile. "I don't want to take any more of your time, especially since I just remembered I've got a conference call."

She glanced briefly at her brother. "You know. With those bastards I pander to. If you'll all excuse me, gentlemen."

She picked up her briefcase and walked out of the office and Richard wondered if either of the other men saw the way her fingers trembled on the handle—or the determined lift of her chin as she left the office.

Chapter Eight

After Anna left, the three men sat in silence for a long, awkward moment.

J.D. was the first to break it. He gave Peter a long look. "Next time give me some warning when you're going to beat up on your little sister and I'll make sure I have someone from the E.R. standing by to mop up."

Peter shrugged. "Anna gives as good as she gets. She always has."

His nonchalance about the pain that had been radiating from Anna suddenly infuriated Richard. She was vulnerable in ways her family refused to see. She always had been.

As hospital counsel, he knew he ought to stay out of the Wilder family squabbles. It was none of his business. But he cared about Anna—he always had—and he couldn't quite force himself to stay quiet.

"She's only trying to do her job," he finally said. "I know the fact that she has that job infuriates you but you didn't have to make it personal, Peter. You did that, she didn't."

Surprise flickered in Peter's gaze at Richard's defense of Anna, then quickly shifted to guilt. "You're right. You're absolutely right."

"This whole takeover attempt would be much easier to fight if Northeastern HealthCare had sent someone else—anyone else—to do their dirty work," he continued. "Anna's presence makes everything feel personal, like the corporation is waging a war against the whole Wilder family, not just the hospital. I'm afraid I got a little carried away. I'm sorry."

"We're not the ones you need to apologize to," J.D. pointed out to his future brother-in-law quietly.

Peter sighed. "I know. Things are just…complicated with Anna. They have been for a long time. But you're right. She didn't deserve that."

He stood and studied Richard with an odd look in his eyes. After a moment he seemed to come to some decision. "Rich, when you're done here with J.D. would you mind stopping by my office for a moment? I need to talk to you about something."

Still annoyed with him for his casual oblivion when it came to his sister's feelings—and even more annoyed with himself for caring so much about something that wasn't any of his business—Richard wasn't in the mood to be cooperative.

"Sorry. I don't do prenuptial contracts."

Peter gave a bark of surprised laughter. "That's not what I needed. Just stop by if you have time."

* * *

An hour later, his curiosity at fever pitch, Richard made his way through the hospital to Peter's office.

"He's with a patient," the receptionist told him. "Do you mind waiting for a few minutes?"

He had a million things to do but was too curious to leave without some clue as to what Peter could possibly want with him.

Only a few moments passed before Peter joined him. "Thanks for stopping in. I could use some advice."

"You do know I don't handle malpractice cases, either, right?"

Peter laughed. "Wrong again. What I really could use is a little insight from a friend."

Richard raised an eyebrow.

"Specifically, I need advice from a friend of Anna's," Peter added, further confusing him.

He shifted in his seat. "I haven't seen Anna in years, until she came back to town a few weeks ago."

"Neither have I. Not really. But you were friends with her before she left town, right?"

More than friends, but he wasn't about to confide that little detail to her older brother. "Yes," he said warily.

"And Bethany said she saw the two of you together the other day and you still seemed...friendly."

He wracked his brain trying to remember his encounter with Anna the day she had been having lunch with Bethany. "Since she's been back in Walnut River, I've had some interactions with her in an official capacity," he finally said. *Mostly official, anyway.* "I'm not sure how much help I'll be, but I can certainly try."

Peter blew out a breath. "If nothing else, I know I

can at least trust you to keep what I'm about to tell you confidential."

"Of course. What's this about, Peter?"

Peter hesitated for a moment then reached to unlock a desk drawer. He pulled out a slim black folder, from which he extracted a legal-sized white envelope.

"I have a letter to Anna from our father. I received it as executor of his will and I've been trying to figure out what to do with it ever since."

Richard might not have seen Anna until recently, but just from their few interactions, he could tell she still grieved for James. He knew she regretted the stilted relationship and the unresolved business between them before his death.

"Your father has been gone for six months. Why haven't you given it to her before this?"

"When would I have the chance? Anna has done her best to stay away from Walnut River and the family during that six months. Hell, she barely stayed long enough for the funeral. I didn't receive the letter until after she left, and I was still trying to figure out what to do with it when we found out Anna was working for Northeastern HealthCare."

He said the last words like a bitter epithet. Richard remembered how Peter had goaded her earlier in J.D.'s office and the disdain he hadn't bothered to conceal, and his temper heated up a notch.

"What does it matter who she works for? If your father wanted her to read that letter, you have no right to keep it from her, either legally or morally."

"I wish it were that clear-cut. My father didn't make it that easy on me. He left the decision completely up to me. In the cover letter he included with it, he said if I felt she was better off not knowing what it contains, I should burn the letter."

The heat of his temper cooled slightly at Peter's obvious turmoil, though his curiosity ratcheted up another level. "But you haven't burned it, even though Anna works for, in your words, the enemy."

"I haven't burned it. No. Some part of me knows she needs to read it. I just...I don't know how she's going to react. I barely know her anymore, Richard. I wonder if I ever did."

Richard had wondered the same thing about his own relationship with Anna. But he was stunned to realize as he sat in her brother's office that his feelings for her hadn't died. They had only been lying dormant inside him, like spring crocuses, waiting for a chance to break free of the frozen ground.

What the hell was he supposed to do with that? He didn't want to care about her. What possible good would ever come of it, when he was certain she couldn't wait to return to New York and the brilliant business career waiting for her there?

"What's in the letter?" he finally asked.

Peter stared down at the envelope for a long moment and his reluctance was in direct contrast to the vocal, outspoken man who had taken on his sister earlier in J.D.'s office.

"I need your vow of confidentiality first. No matter what, you cannot tell a soul."

"Of course."

"I'll read you the cover letter. That explains everything."

Five minutes later, Richard sat back in his chair, reeling from the information in the letter, from James Wilder's confession that Anna was truly his daughter, conceived during a brief affair with a nurse years ago.

"You have to tell her," he said into the long silence. "You can't keep this from her. She has a right to know."

"You know her, Richard, at least better than I do. How do you think she'll react?"

He thought of Anna and the vulnerability she worked so hard to conceal from the world. "I can't answer that. Stunned, certainly. Overwhelmed. Perhaps angry. Wouldn't you be?"

"Yes. It's a shocker, all right. I've known for six months and I still can't believe it." Peter paused. "I know I probably sound like a cold-hearted bastard here but I have to consider the timing and the possible fallout. In light of the bid to take over the hospital and the vote next week, how do you think this information might impact Anna's role in that bid?"

"I have no idea!"

"What's your best guess? I see things happening one of two ways. Either she might lean more toward our side or, being Anna, she might be more determined than ever to win in some kind of twisted payback against our father for not telling her."

Richard thought of the woman he was coming to know—a woman who could read bedtime stories to a five-year-old with sweetness and affection and then turn shrewdly determined about her career.

She was complex and intriguing, which was a big part of her appeal, he realized.

"I honestly can't answer that, Peter. Why would you think I would have any idea what Anna will do? I told you I barely know her."

"You've got an uncanny knack for gauging people's

behavior. I've seen you in action as you've helped Phil with hospital legal issues. I figured since you and Anna were friends before, you might have a guess."

"Our friendship was over a long time ago. We're both different people now."

"But taking history into account and judging by what you've observed since she's been back, what's your gut telling you?"

"I think none of that matters. It's irrelevant. You need to tell her what's in that letter, regardless of how it might impact the merger. This isn't about the hospital. It's a family matter."

Peter gazed at Richard for a moment then sighed. "I was afraid you would say something like that."

"She deserves to know, Peter. You know she does."

"You're right. I need to tell her as soon as possible. I've put it off too long."

He sighed again, looking not at all thrilled by the prospect. "I don't look forward to it. A hell of a mess my father left, isn't it?"

"Yes. He should have told her himself. This shouldn't be your responsibility."

Peter's laugh was gruff. "An understatement. He took the coward's way out. The only time in his life, I think, that he didn't step up and do what had to be done. I guess my biggest mistake the last six months has been following in his footsteps, at least where Anna is concerned. Thanks, Richard, for the time and for the advice. You have definitely helped put things in perspective for me."

"No problem. Consider it an early wedding gift."

Peter gave a distracted smile and showed him out. As Richard walked through the hospital and to his car he was still stunned by the revelation—and even more stunned by the baffling mix of emotions churning through him toward Anna.

He definitely still had feelings for her. Why else would he be consumed with this warmth and sympathy and something else, something soft and fragile that scared the hell out of him?

Anna was finally back in her rented duplex, wearing her most comfortable jeans and a T-shirt, barefoot, with Lilli curled at her feet, chewing her favorite squeaky toy.

Unfortunately, instead of relaxing, she was getting berated by her boss.

Alfred Daly was hundreds of miles away in Manhattan, probably gazing out the vast window of his office at the peons below who walked the city streets. But despite the distance between them, the man still had the power to make her feel as if she had shrunk several inches since the moment the phone call began.

"Tell me, when are you presenting your report to the hospital board of directors?"

She knew he knew such a significant detail, probably right down to the second, but she played along with him.

"Wednesday at five. They're expected to vote Thursday and give their final recommendation to the mayor and city council later that day."

"And you still believe the vote is too close to call?"

"The board is evenly split, as it has been since we first presented our offer. I believe we're making some progress, though. I think at least one or two of the maybe's have moved toward our camp."

Not without a great deal of wheeling and dealing on her part, but she left that unspoken.

"I certainly hope so. That's why you're there, Miss Wilder."

"Yes, sir."

He didn't mention the threat that had been hanging over her head since the day he had ordered her to come to Walnut River and make the merger happen, though it was uppermost in her mind.

If she failed—if the merger vote did not go their way—Anna knew she would be scrambling to find a new job. Not the end of the world, maybe, but she would find it devastating to start over elsewhere. She had worked too hard at NHC to see it all trickle away because of her stubborn, idealistic family members and their behind-the-scenes opposition.

By the time Daly finished his diatribe fifteen minutes later, Anna realized she had downed half a roll of Tums.

"I want that report no later than noon tomorrow. It's too important to send via e-mail so I want you to upload it directly onto my private server," he snapped.

He gave her a password and username, then hung up with one more dire warning about what would happen if she failed to close the deal.

No pressure, Al. Geez.

Anna hung up the phone and gazed into space, feeling as if she stood at the foot of Mount Everest.

She was on her own here and had been charged with achieving the impossible. Worse, she had just been forcefully reminded that her career hung in the balance if she failed.

Alfred Daly had begun to take the Walnut River General merger personally. She wasn't sure why it was so important to him but she sensed he would not take defeat well. He wanted this hospital and was pulling out all the stops to make it happen.

Suddenly, the doorbell rang, and Lilli bounded to the door, yipping away and jerking Anna from her grim contemplation of an unemployment line in her immediate future. She was not at all in the mood for unexpected company.

After twenty minutes on the phone with her boss, what she really needed was a stiff drink and a long soak in the tub.

Or perhaps both.

The doorbell rang again and Anna jerked the door open, ready to blast away, but the words died in her throat.

Of all the entire population of Walnut River, the last two people she would have expected to find standing on her doorstep on a Friday night were her brother Peter and his fiancée, especially after her altercation with him earlier.

Her day only needed this to go from lousy, straight past miserable, into sheer purgatory.

"Peter…Bethany… What brings you here?"

She could barely even look at her brother. All she could think about was her own immature reaction to him earlier. All her plans to be cool and in control around her family had dissolved with a few harsh words from him. Instead of showing off her logic and business acumen, she had ended up running away like a twelve-year-old girl escaping to the bathroom during gym class to hide her tears.

She wanted to come up with some glib comment, something cool and nonchalant, but the impulse died when she saw his solemn expression.

She instantly forgot about their altercation. "Peter! What is it? What's wrong? Has something happened to David or Ella?"

Peter shook his head. "No. Nothing like that."

"What is it, then?"

For the first time in her memory he appeared to be at a loss for words as he gazed at her mutely.

"May we come in?" Bethany finally asked.

"Oh. Of course. Come in." She held the door open and they walked inside.

Lilli sniffed their ankles for a moment then returned to her chew toy.

"What a darling dog," Bethany said with a smile, and Anna decided she had been right to instinctively like her brother's fiancée. She seemed to have a definite knack for putting people at ease in difficult circumstances.

In fact, right now Anna was quite certain she liked Peter's fiancée more than she liked her brother.

"Come in. Sit down."

"I hope we weren't disturbing you."

"No."

She didn't think Peter would appreciate knowing that she had just finished talking to her boss at NHC so she decided to keep that particular bit of information to herself, especially in light of Peter's obvious unease.

"Can I get you something to drink?" she asked, doing a mental inventory of the meager contents of her larder.

"Nothing for me," Bethany said.

Peter sighed. "I could use a drink right now, but it's probably better if I keep a clear head."

Anna narrowed her gaze at him. "All right, what's going on, Peter? You're freaking me out."

"I'm sorry. I just… Now that I'm here, I don't know how to start."

"I've always found the beginning's as good a place as any," Anna answered.

It was advice they'd all heard from their mother many times and Peter must have recognized one of Alice's familiar axioms. He gave a fleeting smile and she was struck again by his resemblance to their father.

"First of all, I owe you an apology."

She blinked, not at all used to seeing her self-assured oldest brother look so wary.

"I was out of line today at the hospital. Richard Green ripped into me after you left for making things personal and he was exactly right. I said things I shouldn't have today and I apologize. It's just…a little hard for me to watch the little sister I love taking the other side on an issue I care so passionately about."

Warmth soaked through her and Anna didn't know what stunned her more—that Peter said he loved her or that Richard would stand up to defend her.

He had taken her brother to task? She would have liked to have seen it, even though she had a tough time believing it.

"Your apology is not necessary, Peter, but thank you," she said. "You came all the way over here just to tell me you were sorry?"

"Not completely."

He glanced at Bethany and some unspoken signal passed between them, something private and personal that made Anna feel excluded—and envious. She didn't miss the way Bethany slipped her hand in his, or the way Peter seemed to grow a little calmer at the gesture.

"I have something for you," her brother finally said. "Something I should have given you months ago."

He appeared to be empty-handed and Anna gazed at him, baffled. "What is it?"

Peter slid a hand to the inside pocket of his jacket and retrieved an envelope. "Um, Dad left you a letter. It came to me since I'm executor of his estate."

Instantly, joy and anger warred within her—joy that she might have one more message from the father she missed and anger at her brother's high-handedness. "You're just getting around to giving it to me? Dad's been gone for six months!"

"You make it sound so easy. I wish it were. Dad left it up to me whether to give it to you or not, which was a hell of a position to find myself in, especially when you were making yourself scarce."

He held the letter still and she had to fight the urge to snatch it out of his hand and order him out of her house.

"You knew how to find me."

"I did. But you didn't seem to want to have anything to do with us. You couldn't leave fast enough after the funeral. You wouldn't even let me give you a ride some-where. And then we found out you were working for Northeastern HealthCare. You should have told us, Anna."

"Don't make this about me and my choices, Peter. Yes, I should have told you about my job. I was wrong to keep it from the family. But that didn't give you the right to withhold something like this from me."

"No. You're right. I should have given the letter to you long ago. I should have driven to the city and tracked you down at your office if I had to, and I'm sorry I didn't. But I'm here now. Do you want it or not?"

"Peter." Bethany said his name, only that, but it appeared to be enough to center him.

He drew in a deep breath and dragged a hand through his hair in a gesture that again reminded her of their father.

"I'm sorry," he said again. "Here it is. Whatever you want to do. It's out of my hands now."

Chapter Nine

Anna's stomach suddenly clenched with nerves and she wasn't at all sure she wanted to take the letter from Peter's outstretched hand.

What would her father have written in a letter that he couldn't have told her to her face?

Did she really want to know?

The three of them froze in an awkward tableau and the moment dragged out, longer and longer. Finally she drew in a breath and took it from him, though she was still reluctant to open it.

Her name was written on the front in her father's sloping, elegant script. By the weight of the envelope, she guessed it was maybe two or three pages long. No more than that, but it felt oddly heavy, almost burdensome.

She had the strangest premonition that once she read what her father had written in the letter, her life would never be the same. This was one of those before-and-after moments—everything after would be different than it was right at this instant.

She had no idea why she was so certain—maybe the gravity in Peter's eyes.

"Do you know what it's about?" she asked, though she thought she knew the answer.

His mouth tightened and he nodded. "I haven't read it but he included another letter to me explaining what was in it. I think it's safe to say what he has to tell you is…unexpected."

She nodded but still couldn't bring herself to open it.

"We can wait while you read it," Peter said after another moment. "You might have questions. Scratch that. You will have questions. I can't answer many of them but I'll do what I can."

Finally she knew she couldn't sit much longer, putting off the inevitable. She carefully slid a finger under the flap of the sealed envelope and pulled out the sheets of paper.

The lines of her father's handwriting turned wobbly and blurred for a moment. She blinked quickly, horrified that she might cry in front of her brother.

She thought she had come to terms with his death—and the distance between them the last few years. Though she did her best to contain it, a single tear slid past her defenses. She swiped at it, hoping Peter didn't see. But to her surprise, a moment later, he sat next to her on the sofa and Bethany sat on her other side.

"Take your time," Bethany murmured, with a comforting arm around her shoulder. She didn't know what might be in the letter but she was suddenly enormously grateful for their presence and the strength she drew from having them near.

They had taken time from their wedding preparations to be here for her, she realized with some wonder.

She drew in another shaky breath and smoothed a hand down the paper.

"My dearest Anna," her father's letter began.

I have written this letter in my head a hundred times over the years. A thousand. Each time, the words seem to tangle in my mind and eventually I stopped trying. This time I must press forward, no matter how difficult I find the task.

I must first tell you how very proud I am of you for what you have done with your life. I may not have agreed with your decision to leave medical school—I still believe you would have made an excellent physician. You were always so compassionate and loving.

But over the years I have come to accept that you had to chart your own destiny, and I will say now what I should have said eight years ago. I believe you made the right choice to leave medical school. Your heart was never in it, something I refused to see back then. One of my biggest regrets in life is that I was not the sort of father I should have been to you. I should have listened to your worries and fears instead of trying so hard to crowd you onto the path I wanted for you.

I did try to be a good father to you. Perhaps I tried too hard. I wanted so much for you to feel you belonged. I know things were not always easy for you. I could see the lost look in your eyes when you would see one of your siblings on your mother's lap or having a bedtime story with her and I always tried to rush in to fill the void.

My dear, I ask you not to judge Alice too harshly. She was a wonderful woman who endured more than you can ever guess, more than any woman should. I always suspected she had guessed the truth about you, the truth I dared not tell her.

She never said anything and I know she loved you in her way but surely you sensed she treated you differently than Peter or David or Ella.

Neither of us ever spoke of it—afraid, I think, to upset the fragile peace we had achieved. But time is no longer my friend. When a man reaches a certain age, he must come face to face with his own mortality. I don't want this secret to die with me.

I only ask that as you read this, you do not judge me too harshly. Please remember how much I have always loved you.

The truth is, I have lied to you for all these years about how you came to be part of our family. The story about finding you on the steps of the hospital is true. But missing in that tale are certain significant details.

She paused to turn the page, still vaguely aware of Peter and Bethany on either side of her, bolstering her.

I was the one who "found" you, yes, but only because that was the prearranged plan between me and your mother. Your birth mother.

I'm sure it will shock you to find out I knew all

along who she was. It wasn't some unknown mystery woman who left you, but a nurse at Walnut River General. See, Anna, you are my daughter. Not only through adoption but in every other way.

She inhaled sharply and lifted shocked eyes to Peter, who was watching her through her father's solemn eyes. She jerked her gaze away from him and focused on the letter again.

Please, I beg you again, don't judge me too harshly. I had one moment of indiscretion during the depths of Alice's depression, when she had retreated to a dark and terrible place. Monica, your birth mother, showed me great kindness and compassion and in a moment of weakness, I went against every standard I have ever believed in. She was not at fault, the blame was wholly mine. I cannot regret it. I know I should, but without that moment of weakness, I never would have had the great honor and privilege of being your father.

Anna realized she was gripping the letter so hard she was afraid she would tear it. She forced her grasp to relax as she fought back tears. A moment later, a handkerchief appeared in front of her and she took it from Peter but still didn't allow the tears to fall.

I'm sure you're curious about your birth mother and why she would choose to give you up. She was a wonderful woman, kind and generous, but she wasn't at all prepared to be a mother, especially not on her own. I know that leaving you with me was the hardest decision she ever made, but she knew that as a Wilder, you would have opportunities she couldn't provide on her own.

I'm sorry to say she is gone now. She died not long after your birth when the small plane she was flying in crashed, but I am certain her last thoughts were of you.

Our actions were done out of love for you, Anna. Please don't forget that. Even the deception I have maintained over the years was out of love and the enduring hope that you would find acceptance and stability in our family.

I am sorry for the years of deception. I should have told you earlier, I see that now. I only pray that someday you will forgive me for the magnitude of the lie.

I love you, my darling Anna. I have been proud to call you my own every moment of your life.
Your devoted father
James Wilder

She finished the letter and sat stunned for a long moment, the pages dangling from her fingers.

She didn't know what to think, what to feel.

She was not some anonymous orphan, as she had believed for so many years. She was James Wilder's daughter, conceived during a brief affair with a nurse at the hospital.

Her father's daughter, in every possible way.

She felt numb, dazed, and couldn't seem to work her brain around the implications.

"You...knew about this?" she finally said, her jaw so achy and tight the words were hard to get out.

Peter nodded. "I told you, he left me a cover letter explaining everything. I've known for months, I just haven't known how to tell you."

"How could he?"

The words were wrenched from her and she didn't know what she meant—her father's infidelity in the first place or the years of deception upon deception from the man she had always considered the most scrupulously honest she had ever known.

Peter sighed. "You don't remember what Mom went through during those terrible days of her depression, before she found the right combo of meds to control it. I do. I remember it vividly. I was nine and I can remember days when I was afraid to come home from school, because I didn't know what I would find. It was horrible. The medication they gave her made it worse. She was barely there and when she came to herself, she would rage and scream at Dad for hours."

She closed her eyes, feeling battered and achy and still fighting tears. If she let them out, she was afraid she wouldn't be able to stop.

"Do— Do Ella and David know?"

He shook his head. "Bethany knows and I've confided in two others, seeking advice—a social worker and friend at the hospital and more recently, Richard Green."

She stared. "Richard knows? And he said nothing to me?"

"I only told him today after I saw you in J.D.'s office. I swore him to secrecy."

So Richard hadn't betrayed her. She found some solace in that.

"Will you tell them? David and Ella, I mean?"

Peter shook his head. "That's your decision. If you want them to know, I can tell them but perhaps you should be the one to do it. And if you decide to say nothing, I will back you up."

He paused, appearing to choose his words carefully. "Things are difficult between us all right now. I would only ask that if you tell them, you don't do it out of spite or anger."

His words were a blunt reminder of the rift between her and her siblings, of the chasm she had no idea how to cross.

She forced a smile that didn't feel at all genuine. "Always the protector, aren't you, Peter?"

He studied her solemnly. "Of you as well, Anna."

She didn't know how to respond to that and the tears seemed even closer to the surface. Bethany seemed to sense the fissures in her control. She squeezed Anna's arm.

"The wedding rehearsal dinner is next Friday," she said softly. "It would mean a great deal to us if you would be there. Will you come?"

Would she even still be in town? she wondered. The hospital board of directors was set to vote on Thursday and everything would be decided by then.

Still, she was deeply grateful suddenly for Bethany's freely offered friendship.

"I'll try," she managed.

Bethany gave her a hug. "That's all we can ask," she said.

To her shock, Peter hugged her next. "I would say welcome to the family, but it doesn't seem quite appropriate since you've been my sister for thirty years."

Somehow she managed a smile, though it felt watery and thin. "Thank you for bringing this, even though you didn't want to. I understand your hesitation a little better now."

"Dad never should have kept it from you and I shouldn't have either for this long."

He paused, then embraced her again. "When the shock wears off, I hope you will see this as a good thing. You've always been one of us, Anna. Blood or not. But maybe knowing you share our blood will help you see that more clearly."

She nodded and showed them out.

When they left, Lilli gazed at her quizzically. Anna re-read the letter, still fighting tears, while the walls of her bland, boring, temporary home seemed to be closing in on her, crowding her, smothering her.

She suddenly needed to escape from the thick emotions squeezing her chest, stealing her breath, choking her throat.

And she knew exactly where she needed to go.

"Good night, kiddo. You be good for Grandma, okay?"

"Dad!" In that single word, Ethan managed to convey all the disgust of a teenager instead of a five-year-old. "You know I always am!"

Richard smiled into the phone. "Of course you are. I love you, bud."

"I love you, too, Dad."

The sweet, pure words put a lump in his throat, as they always did. "Can you put your grandma on the phone again?"

"Okeydokey."

After a moment's silence, his mother picked up the phone.

"Are you really sure you want to do this, Mom? You've had him all day."

"Absolutely." His mother's voice was firm and not at all as exhausted as he might have expected after she had wrangled Ethan for the past ten hours. "You know we've been planning this sleepover for a week. We're camping out. I've got a tent set up in my living room and the sleeping bags are already up. We're going to roast marshmallows in the gas fireplace after I crank up the air conditioning to compensate and I have all the makings of s'mores ready to go. We're going to have a blast."

That was part of the problem, Richard admitted. He hated being excluded. He hadn't seen Ethan since dropping him off at his grandmother's that morning and he missed his son.

Ethan's absence was part of his restlessness, but not all of it. Some had to do with a particular woman he couldn't get out of his mind.

"Thanks, then," he said. "You two have a great time. I'll pick him up tomorrow morning."

"No hurry. We'll probably sleep in."

"Wishful thinking, Mom. Ethan's idea of sleeping in is waiting to jump out of bed until six-forty-five instead of six-thirty."

His mother laughed. "I'll survive. The question is, what will you do with a night to yourself?"

He was so unused to the idea that he found the prospect of an evening without Ethan rather daunting. "I'm slammed with work right now so I'll probably just take advantage of the chance to catch up."

"Booorrring. Can't you think of something better than work? It's Friday night. Why don't you go out and have some fun? Call up one of those girls on your BlackBerry and head out for a night on the town."

The only females on his BlackBerry were clients or associates, but he decided his mother didn't really need to know that particular piece of information.

"Interesting idea," he murmured. "I doubt it will happen but I'll certainly add it to the list of possibilities."

His mother was quiet for a moment. When she spoke, her voice held a surprising degree of concern. "I worry about you, Richard. You're a wonderful father, but your world has become only about work and about your son. You need to take time for yourself once in awhile. Go have a little fun. Grab a little spontaneity in your life."

Richard frowned. Where was this coming from? Okay, so he didn't have much of a social life. But when, exactly, was he supposed to find the time for one while being a full-time father?

He opened his mouth to answer, but before he could, the doorbell chimed through the empty house.

Relief flooded him at the convenient excuse to end the conversation. "I've gotta go, Mom. Somebody's at the door."

"Oh, good. Maybe it's a hot girl looking for a little action."

A strangled laugh escaped him. "Wouldn't that be an odd twist of fate?"

"Stranger things have happened."

"If I were you, I wouldn't hold my breath. Have fun sleeping on the floor."

He hung up and hurried to answer the door. In light of the conversation with his mother, he couldn't have been more shocked to find Anna Wilder on his doorstep.

"Anna!"

"I…didn't know where else to go."

His initial surprise shifted quickly to concern. Her eyes were hollow and her face looked ashen in the pale glow of his porch light.

She was holding an envelope in her hand and he knew instantly that Peter must have given her James's letter.

He only had about half a second for the thought to register before she launched herself into his arms.

He caught her but the momentum pushed them both back into the room. He heard a strangled gasp and then, like a torrent, she began to weep great, heaving sobs, as if she had been waiting for only this moment to unleash them.

He eased down to the sofa and pulled her onto his lap.

He held her for a long time, until the sobs finally began to subside. She was trembling, little shivers that broke his heart, and he tightened his arms. After a moment, she let out a deep breath and struggled to regain control, and he relaxed his hold a little.

"I'm sorry." Her voice sounded raspy. "I'm so sorry. I didn't mean to…I never intended to come here and break down like this. I just…I had to talk to someone and I didn't know where else to go."

"I'm glad you came here."

"I feel so stupid. I don't know what happened. I saw you and suddenly it all just seemed too much."

He was honored and humbled that she trusted him enough to let him see beyond the cool veneer she showed to the world. "Do you want to talk about it?"

"You mean blubbering all over your shirt for twenty minutes isn't enough torture?"

It *was* torture having her in his arms, but not the way she meant. Despite the toll it was taking on his control, he wasn't about to relinquish this chance to hold her, in any capacity.

"I'm guessing you talked to Peter."

She sighed. "Yes. He said he talked to you earlier today and told you about the letter from my father."

"He did."

"Then you know the truth. That James Wilder is my father. My true father, not just my adopted one."

"A bit of a shock, wasn't it?"

She gave a short, bitter laugh. "It changes everything I thought I knew about myself."

"You're still the same person, Anna. Finding out your genetic blueprint doesn't change thirty years of living."

She was silent for a moment, her cheek still pressed against his chest. She didn't seem inclined to leave his lap and he certainly wasn't in any hurry to let her go.

"I have always believed I stood on the outside of the Wilder family circle. My mother—Alice—didn't exactly push me out but I never truly felt welcome, even though James did everything possible to make me feel I belonged. Now I understand why."

"She knew you were his child?"

"My father said in the letter he thought she must have guessed but they never discussed it."

"It must have been terribly difficult for her if she did suspect. To keep her head high while she raised her husband's illegitimate child."

"Yes. It explains so much about…everything."

To his regret, she finally slid from his lap and sat beside him on the couch, her hands tightly folded on her lap.

Though he knew a little distance was probably a wise thing right about now, Richard couldn't prevent himself from reaching out and covering her clasped hands with his. After a moment, she gripped his tightly.

"You know, I think he tried to tell me several times over the years, in an oblique kind of way," she said. "The summer I…left, when I dropped out of med school and everything, I tried to tell him how unhappy I was. I told him straight out that I was afraid I just didn't have the Wilder gene for medicine. I can remember him saying in that sturdy, no-nonsense voice of his, 'Don't let me hear you say that again. You're as much a Wilder as the rest of my children!' I thought it was simply another effort to make me feel I belonged in the family."

"What will you do now?"

She closed her eyes and leaned against the sofa. Her color had returned, he was pleased to see. Despite the crying jag, she was so beautiful he couldn't seem to look away.

"I don't know. Peter says he hasn't told Ella and David. He seems to think I'll blab it to them out of spite over the hospital merger."

Despite her glib tone, he could hear the hurt underscoring her words and his heart ached for her. He couldn't help himself, and he pulled her into his arms again.

"You'll figure it all out, Anna. I know it must feel like an atomic bomb has just dropped into your lap, but when you think about it, what has really changed?"

"Everything!"

"Maybe you found out your father had some human weaknesses after all. But your siblings are still your siblings, just as they've always been. You might all be going through a rough time right now with the hospital merger but they still love you."

She sighed against his chest. "I feel like everything I thought I knew about myself is a lie."

"It's not, Anna. Not at all. What's different right now than it was a few hours ago? You're still a bright beautiful woman who loves her dog and is kind to little boys and who still makes my heart pound."

Her gaze flashed to his for one breathless moment before he surrendered to the inevitable and kissed her.

Chapter Ten

Anna closed her eyes and leaned into Richard, trying to absorb his strength.

She needed him. For comfort, yes, but for so much more. She found a peace in his arms that she had never known anywhere else.

Though she had dated in the eight years she'd been away, she had never cared enough about any of those men to take a relationship beyond the casual to this ultimate step.

This had never felt right with anyone but Richard. He was the only man she had ever made love to.

She wondered what he would say if she told him that and decided to keep the information to herself for now.

She wrapped her arms around his neck with the oddest sensation that this was where she belonged. Right here, with his mouth firm and insistent against hers, his masculine scent filling her senses, his hard strength against her.

Here, in his arms, she didn't feel disconnected or off kilter. It didn't matter whether she was the odd Wilder out or James Wilder's illegitimate daughter. She had nothing to prove here—she knew exactly who she was when Richard Green kissed her. Everything else faded to nothing.

He deepened the kiss, until tiny sparks raced up and down her nerve endings, until her thighs trembled and every inch of her skin ached for his touch.

"You taste exactly like I remember," he murmured.

"How?" Was that breathy, aroused voice hers, she wondered with some amazement. What happened to the brisk and businesslike woman she had always considered herself?

"Like every delicious, decadent, sinful dessert ever created. Sweet and heady and intoxicating. That's you."

His words ignited more heat and she kissed him fiercely, reveling in his sharp intake of breath, in the tremble of his hands on the bare skin above the waistband of her jeans.

He traced designs on the sensitive skin at her waist for long, intoxicating moments, then finally moved to the buttons of her white shirt.

A wild hunger for his touch bubbled and seethed deep inside her and she arched against his hand, needing him with a steady, fiery ache.

He opened the buttons of her shirt and touched her through the lacy fabric of her bra and she found the sight of his sun-browned hand against her pale skin the most erotic thing she'd ever seen.

She arched against him, wanting more. Wanting everything. For long moments, they kissed and touched, until nothing else mattered but this moment.

"I'm going to have to stop." His voice was raspy with

need. "I'm afraid I have no self-control where you're concerned."

"Take it from me. Self-control is overrated," she murmured, her voice a breathy purr.

He closed his eyes for a moment. When he opened them again, they were dark with passion. "I can't take advantage of you, Anna. You're upset. This isn't really what you want."

"You couldn't be more wrong. This is exactly what I want."

He looked torn between desire and his sense of duty and she decided to take the decision out of his hands. She kissed him hard, wrapping her arms around him tightly and savoring the strength against her.

He groaned. "I can't fight you and myself at the same time."

"Then don't," she said.

He kissed her again, fierce and possessive, and her stomach trembled with anticipation. It wouldn't be the same magic she remembered from eight years ago, she warned herself. It couldn't be.

She was only half-right.

It wasn't the same. It was better. Much, much better.

They kissed their way down the hall to his bedroom and she had a vague impression of bold masculine colors and a massive bed before Richard began to undress her with a soft gentleness that nearly made her weep.

She was in love with him.

The realization washed through her, not with the punishing force of a tidal wave, but like a sweet cleansing rain on parched desert soil.

It was terribly difficult not to blurt the words out right then but she choked them back. He didn't want to hear them. Not now. She had hurt him eight years ago, he had said as much. He might let her into his arms and his bed but somehow she knew finding her way back into his heart wouldn't be nearly as easy.

She put the fear away for now as she helped him out of his clothes and then she forgot her fears, lost in the sheer wonder of having all those muscles to explore.

They kissed and touched for a long time, until both of them were breathing raggedly, their hearts pounding.

At last, when she didn't think she could endure another moment, he grabbed a condom from the bedside table and entered her, and she again had to choke back her words of love as sensation after sensation poured over her.

She pressed a hard kiss to his mouth, desperate to show him with her lips and her body how she felt about him, even if she didn't quite feel she could say the words yet.

He gripped her hands tightly as he moved deeply inside her and she cried out his name, stunned at her wild hunger. She arched into him, desperate and achy.

She couldn't wait another second, another instant. Sensing how close she was to the edge, he reached between their bodies and touched her at the apex of her thighs and the world exploded in a wild burst of color and heat and sensation.

While her body still shivered and hummed, he pushed even deeper inside her, deeper than she would have thought possible, then groaned out her name as he found his own release.

He held her while they floated back to earth together and she mouthed the words she couldn't say aloud against his chest.

"What did you say?" he asked softly.

She shook her head, her hair brushing his skin. "Wow," she lied. "Just wow."

He laughed softly and pulled her closer and she wondered how she had ever found the strength—or the stupidity—to walk away from this eight years ago.

He awoke to the pale light of early morning filtering through his window and an odd sense of peace.

The sensation was unfamiliar enough that it compelled him to slide a little further into consciousness. Most mornings, he jumped out of bed ready for the day's many battles—from his regular tussle with Ethan over breakfast cereals to pondering the many things on his to-do list.

This morning, his limbs were loose and relaxed, his thoughts uncharacteristically still.

While he was trying to piece together why that might be, a sexy feminine scent drifted through the air from the pillow beside him, and he saw an unfamiliar indentation with a few long blond hairs against the pillowcase.

The memories came flowing back—of Anna in his arms, her mouth eager, her body soft and responsive.

He closed his eyes, reliving the incredible night they had just shared. It had been more than he would ever have imagined. Much more. He had never known such tenderness, such overwhelming sweetness.

They had made love three times and each time had been more intense than the time before.

And now she was gone.

He opened his eyes, not quite sure why he was so certain of it. Her clothes were gone and some instinct told him he didn't need to search his house to know he wouldn't find her.

He couldn't say he was really surprised. Saddened, maybe, but not really surprised.

The bleak inevitability of it still made him want to throw on a pair of jeans and tear off after her, chase her down at her apartment and confront her, but he checked the impulse. What the hell good would that accomplish, besides making him look like an idiot?

He sat up, his emotions a tight hot tangle in his chest. He was in love with her—a thousand times more now, this morning, than he had been eight years ago. Those had been fledgling, newborn feelings.

This, what he felt right now, was powerful and strong.

Too bad for him, but if their history ran true, Anna was likely to whip out a twenty gauge shotgun and blast his heart right out of the sky.

He didn't learn his lesson very well with her, did he? He was either a masochist or he had no sense of self-preservation whatsoever.

Anna just wasn't emotionally available.

She couldn't make it more clear to him if she took out a damn billboard right outside his office.

Even when they made love, he could sense she held some part of herself back, something she hid away from him. He didn't know whether that was a protective mechanism from a childhood where she struggled to belong, or if it stemmed from her dedication to her career, but even in his arms she wouldn't let him through that last line of defenses.

He sighed. So much for the relaxed state he'd awakened to. His shoulders now ached with tension and regret.

It was still early, just barely daylight. He wasn't going to lay here and brood, he decided. He had survived having his heart broken by Anna Wilder before. He could certainly do it again. The trick was returning to as normal a life as possible, forcing himself to go through the motions until the vicious ache in his heart began to fade.

He was getting to be an expert.

When she had left before, the only thing that had saved him had been law school. He had thrown himself into his final two years, until he didn't have room in his brain to think about anything else but tort reforms and trial transcripts.

At least now he had Ethan to distract him.

A good, hard run before he went to his mother's to collect his son for the day would be an excellent place to start picking up the pieces of his world, he decided. A little physical activity would be just the thing to burn off this restlessness suddenly churning through him.

Ten minutes later, dressed in jogging shorts and a T-shirt, he was heading out the front door when he spotted an envelope on the coffee table in the living room.

He saw her name on the front and realized this must be the letter from her father. His mind flashed to the night before, to her coming through the door and into his arms. She had been holding it then. Sometime during the wild storm of emotion that came after when she had wept in his arms, she must have dropped it on the table.

He was going to have to return it to her, which meant he would have to see her again.

Sooner, rather than later.

He grimaced, gazing malevolently at the envelope. Getting over her again would be a hell of a lot easier if he didn't have to face her every damn time he turned around.

* * *

She was an idiot.

Anna sat in her living room, Lilli curled up at her feet and her laptop humming on the coffee table in front of her as she tried to focus on work instead of the delectable image of Richard, naked and masculine, as she'd left him a few hours earlier.

Walking away from that bedroom and out of his house had been the single hardest thing she had ever done.

She had stood watching him sleep for a long time in the soft light of early morning, trying to force herself to go.

With one arm thrown over his head, his features relaxed and youthful in sleep, he had been so gorgeous that she had wanted nothing more than to climb right back into his bed and never leave.

She sighed, gazing at her computer until the words blurred.

She was in love with him.

It was one thing to face such a thought when she was in his arms, when his body was warm and hard against hers. It was something else entirely in the cold unforgiving light of morning, when she couldn't escape the harsh reality that they had no possible future together.

She had destroyed any chance of that eight years ago, when she made the fatal decision that proving herself to her family was more important than following her heart.

It had been a colossal mistake. She could see that now.

Richard didn't trust her enough to love her. Even when he had been deep inside her, she had seen the doubt shadowing his gaze, the edge of distance he was careful to maintain.

She deserved it. She had hurt him by leaving, more than she had ever imagined.

The night she had shared dinner with him at his house, he had told her with blunt and brutal honesty that he had only dated Ethan's mother because she had reminded him of Anna.

He had offered her his heart eight years ago and she had callously refused it. She supposed it was only right and just, somehow, that now she would be the one to bleed.

She stared at her computer for a long time then glanced at the clock. She had promised Mr. Daly her report would be posted on his private server by noon, which gave her only an hour to finish up.

Compartmentalizing her heartache was almost as hard as walking out of Richard's house, but she forced herself to focus on work with the harsh reminder that she only had a few days left in Walnut River. Either way the board voted, her work here would be done by the end of the week and she could return to the city and the life she had created there.

She quickly input the new numbers from the hospital in her report then went online to access Daly's private server via the instructions he had given her the night before.

It only took a moment to upload her report. Just as she was about to disconnect she spied a folder she had never seen before, labeled WRG/Wilder.

She stared at it for a long moment, a vague foreboding curling through her like ominous wisps of smoke where they didn't belong.

She had no business reading Daly's private files, even if they did have her name on them.

But he had given her the access code to his server,

she reminded herself. Surely he wouldn't have done that if the server contained information he didn't want her to see.

Maybe this was some kind of message to her and he meant for her to see it. Maybe if she didn't read it, he would accuse her of not doing her job somehow. The man could be devious that way.

After another moment of dithering, she surrendered to her curiosity and opened the folder. It contained only one file, she saw, with the initials P.W.

In for a penny, she thought, and clicked to open it....

Ten minutes later, she printed out the document after making her own backup copy. Her hands were shaking so much she could barely move them on the keyboard to disconnect from the server.

She shut down her laptop and folded it closed, then eased back on the sofa. Her stomach roiled as the bagel she'd had that morning seemed to churn around inside her. She pressed a hand to the sudden burning there while her mind whirled with the implications of what she had just read.

She wasn't sure which emotion was stronger inside her right now—outrage at what her superiors planned for the hospital or the deep sense of betrayal that she had been used.

P.W. stood for *Peter Wilder.* That had been abundantly clear the moment she opened the file that turned out to be an internal memo between Daly and his three closest cohorts.

She closed her eyes as snippets of the memo seemed to dance behind her eyelids. *Force out old guard. Bring in cheaper labor. Cut costs and services.*

It was bad enough that NHC planned to do exactly as her siblings claimed, sacrifice patient care for the bottom line. Worse was the way they intended to win this battle, by using her to bring down her siblings, primarily Peter.

Peter Wilder leads the opposition, the memo stated clearly. *Take him out and you'll cut the opponents off at the knees.*

The smear tactics outlined in the memo were brutally ugly, ranging from manufacturing malpractice allegations to planting a patient willing to accuse him of sexual misconduct.

Anna pressed a hand to her mouth, sickened all over again as she remembered her own passionate defense of Northeastern HealthCare, how absolutely certain she had been that the company had the community's needs at heart.

How could she have allowed herself to be so blind?

She thought she had been doing the right thing. For two years, she had bought into the NHC philosophy of providing streamlined medical care to reach the masses. She had wanted to believe in their mission. She had nothing but respect for her direct supervisor, Wallace Jeffers. He had always struck her as a man of integrity and honor.

Not everyone at NHC was like him, she had to admit. Now, as she looked back over two years, she could see times she had turned her head away at practices that might have blurred ethical lines.

She hadn't wanted to see them, she acknowledged now. She had wanted only to focus on her career and climbing as high as she could. Wallace had talked about her succeeding him as vice president of mergers and acquisitions, sometime long in the future, and she had wanted it.

She'd been brought into this project not because of any brilliance on her part, she saw now, but because she was

a Wilder. Alfred Daly seemed to have an almost patho-
logical need to win the NHC merger. He was frustrated
and angry at all the complications and delays the past six
months in what should have been a simple process.

Of course he would use any advantage in front of
him. No doubt he thought her presence would be enough
to distract her family while NHC implemented more nefarious plans.

This memo was dated a few weeks earlier. She read it
again, sick all over again. Were the wheels in motion
already? Was her brother going to be hit any day now with
some kind of trumped-up malpractice suit or an allega-
tion of sexual abuse?

Her honorable upright brother would be devastated by
either option.

"Oh, Lilli. What am I going to do?"

Her dog yapped in response, her head cocked and her
eyes curiously sympathetic.

The dog held her gaze for just an instant before she
suddenly scampered to the door with an excited yip, then
sat vibrating with eagerness, her little body aquiver.

As usual, Lilli was prescient. The doorbell rang an
instant later and Anna groaned, tempted to ignore it and
pretend she wasn't home.

The doorbell rang again, more insistently this time.
Who was she fooling? Her car was in the driveway, and
whoever was out there probably knew she was sitting
here trying to pretend she was invisible.

"Anna?" She heard through the door and closed her
eyes at the sound of Richard's smooth voice.

Who else? She only needed this.

She was even more tempted to ignore the doorbell, but

she just couldn't bring herself to do it. Finally she ramped up her courage and forced herself to wrench open the door.

Sunlight gleamed in his golden hair and he looked gorgeous—sexy and casual in jeans and a polo shirt. She had an instant's image of how she had left him that morning, the sheets tousled at his waist and his muscled chest hard and warm.

Awkwardness at seeing him again temporarily supplanted her dismay over the memo.

A few hours ago, she had been in his arms. She had no experience with this sort of thing and didn't know how to face him.

"Hi," she finally said, her voice throaty.

He nodded, though his stoic expression didn't change.

"Would you…like to come in?"

After a moment, he stepped through the doorway with a reluctance she didn't miss. He stopped for a moment to greet Lilli, who hopped around with infatuated enthusiasm.

"I can't stay," he finally said. "I'm picking Ethan up in an hour. I just wanted to return this. You left it at my house."

He held out a familiar envelope and she stared. She certainly hadn't forgotten the stunning news that she was James's daughter but the letter had completely slipped her mind when she was sneaking away from Richard's bed.

"Oh. Right. Um, thank you."

"You're welcome."

They lapsed into an awkward silence. She wished she could read his expression but he seemed stiff and unapproachable.

"Why did you…"

"Look, I'm sorry I…"

They both spoke to break the silence at the same time and Anna gestured. "You first," she said.

He shrugged. "I just wanted to know why you rushed away this morning without a word. You could have at least nudged me awake to say goodbye."

She flushed, not at all in the mood to talk about this right now after the tumult of the past half hour.

Richard made it sound like she had taken what she wanted from him and then left on her merry way without giving him another thought. It wasn't at all like that, but she could certainly see how he might have been left with that impression.

She couldn't very well tell him she had been terrified by the wild torrent of emotions rushing through her, that she had been almost desperate for the safety of a little distance from him.

"I don't know that I can answer that," she finally said, her voice wary. "I was hoping to avoid this kind of awkwardness. I guess I thought it would be…easier that way."

His mouth hardened. "I wouldn't want you to try something hard."

His words were quiet, which only made them that much more devastating.

"What's that supposed to mean?"

"Nothing. Forget it." He looked toward the door as if he regretted saying anything and wanted to escape.

"No. I'd like to hear what you have to say."

"You sure about that?"

She folded her arms across her chest, though she knew that pitiful gesture would do nothing to protect her heart.

"Yes. Tell me."

"I'm just looking at your track record. You quit medical school because it was too tough for you."

"Not true! I had straight A's my first year. I walked out because I hated it!"

"Fine. You're right. It wasn't tough academically, just emotionally, which for you was even harder. So instead of staying and explaining to your family that you hated it, instead of taking a stand, you chose to run. You were so afraid of your family's reaction that you gave up on *us* before we even had a chance. You've got a track record, at least where I'm concerned, so I guess I wasn't really surprised you walked out this morning. It's what you do. You're good at it."

She managed, just barely, not to sway from the bitter impact of his anger. How dare he? she wanted to say, but the words tangled in her throat. She only had to look at her laptop and that damning memo to know he was right. Absolutely right.

She was a blind, self-absorbed idiot whose actions were threatening her family and her community.

She deserved his condemnation and more. Much more.

Chapter Eleven

He needed to shut the hell up and just leave, pretend the last twelve hours hadn't happened, but Richard couldn't seem to make the words stop coming. "Even as we were making love, I expected you to leave. That doesn't make it hurt any less. That's all I'm saying."

Her features had paled a shade, but in typical Anna fashion, she stiffened her shoulders. "I don't understand. If you have such contempt for me and think I'm such a terrible person, why would you want anything to do with me?"

Though her tone was calm, dispassionate even, he didn't miss the hurt in her eyes, a pain she was trying valiantly to conceal from him.

"I don't think you're a terrible person. Quite the contrary. I wouldn't be—" in love with you, he almost said, but checked himself just in time "—I wouldn't be here if I did. I think you're a brilliant, capable, beautiful woman who doesn't see her own strengths. You don't see yourself as I do, as someone with the ability to cope with anything that comes along. Because you don't see it, you protect yourself by avoiding things you're afraid you can't handle."

She looked as if he had just punched her in the gut and Richard sighed. He needed to just shut the hell up and leave. He tended to forget how vulnerable she was.

He had no business coming here, twisting everything, making it all about her.

"I'd better go. Ethan will be home soon. I just thought you might be looking for your father's letter."

"Thank you."

She didn't meet his gaze and Richard closed his eyes, furious with himself. "Look, I'm sorry. Forget I said anything. I'm just acting like a spoiled brat. I can't have what I want and so I'm blaming everyone in the world but myself."

"What…do you want?"

"Haven't you figured that out yet? I want you. Still. Always."

She blinked those big gorgeous eyes and with a sigh, he stepped forward and pulled her into his arms.

She stood frozen with shock in his arms for just a moment then she seemed to melt against him, her mouth soft and eager against his. Her arms clasped around his neck and he lost himself to the heat that always flared between them.

Was it only because he knew he couldn't have her? he wondered. Was that why each touch, each taste, seemed such a miracle? As if each time might be the last.

He wasn't sure how it happened but she was backed

against the wall, her body wrapped around his, and he was lost in the overwhelming tenderness, unlike anything he had ever known with anyone else.

They kissed for a long time, until finally she sighed against his mouth and he tasted exactly the moment when she started to withdraw.

She slid her mouth away from his and backed away, her eyes wide, slightly dazed, for only a moment before she seemed to blink back to awareness.

"I wish you wouldn't do that."

"What? Kiss you?"

"Confuse me," she said, her voice low. "Distract me. Richard, I can't do this with you. Last night was…"

A mistake. He heard the words, even though she cut off the sentence before she said them.

"I was confused and upset and I—I needed you. I won't deny that. But I shouldn't have stayed. The lines are too blurred. Surely you can see that. You're the hospital attorney and I…"

"And?"

"And things are so complicated right now. I can't even begin to tell you." Her gaze flashed to her laptop behind him. "*Complicated* is an understatement. Right now, I need…I can't afford to be distracted by you. By this."

The words had a painfully familiar ring to them. She was doing it again, damn her.

"I'm sorry," she murmured. "It's just…my life is a mess. The merger. My family. Northeastern HealthCare. Everything."

When would he stop just handing his heart to her and then sit by watching her twist and yank the poor thing into knots?

"You're right. I wouldn't want a little detail like the fact that I'm in love with you distract you from all that other important stuff in your life right now."

He hadn't meant to say that, damn it. The words slipped out of nowhere to hover between them, where they seemed to expand sharply, to grow and morph until they filled the entire room.

"Richard!"

"Forget I said that."

"How can I?"

"I'm sure you'll find a way. Especially since you're so focused on what's really important. The merger. Your family. NHC. Everything."

As he headed for the door, he dislodged some papers from the coffee table. Out of habit, he reached to pick them up to replace them—it wouldn't do to leave a mess, after all, he thought bitterly—then his attention was caught by the top page in his hand.

He shouldn't have read it but a few key phrases leapt out and grabbed his attention. Law school had taught him to read briefs rapidly and digest them just as quickly. It took less than ten seconds to read enough to feel like throwing up.

"What the hell is this?"

She stared at the paper in his hand and he saw the color leach from her face like bones in the sun. She grabbed for the memo. "Nothing. Absolutely nothing."

He held it above his head so she couldn't reach it. Her dog, thinking they were playing some kind of game, yipped besides their feet. "Nothing! You call this nothing?"

Panic twisted her features and she looked like she shared his nausea, so pale and bilious that he might have allowed a twinge of pity if he'd had room for anything else around the disgust.

"It's not what it looks like."

"I hope to hell it's not."

He pulled it down and read it again and had to fight the urge to shove the whole thing down her throat. "Because what it looks like is your master plan to win this merger fight, no matter what the cost. You're planning to sacrifice your own brother for the sake of your damn job!"

"I'm not!"

"What else? *Take Peter Wilder down, any way you can.* That's what the thing says. *With Wilder out of the picture, the opposition will crumble.* How could you? What have you become, Anna?"

If possible, her features paled further but she still lifted her chin. "You're jumping to unfounded conclusions, counselor."

"To hell with that! The proof is right here. How could you?" he asked again. "You're willing to destroy Peter— your own brother—just to win. The job at all costs. Nothing has changed with you, has it?"

She ignored his words, holding out her hand. Her fingers trembled, he realized, but the sight gave him no satisfaction. "Give it to me, Richard. That is an internal Northeastern HealthCare memo. You have no legal access to it. You're an attorney. You know that."

"It was here in plain sight."

"Among my private papers, in a private home. You read it without my permission and now you just need to forget you ever saw it."

She was right, damn it. She was right and there wasn't a thing he could do about it. He handed over the document with bitter reluctance, as all his illusions about her shattered into nothing.

"I don't even know you, do I? I was completely wrong. How could I have been so stupid? You aren't protecting your emotions. You've got none. You're a cold heartless woman who is willing to sell your own family down the river to get your way."

"Richard—"

He shook his head, cutting her off. "I've been in love with an image all these years. You never cared about me. I finally see it. I tried to convince myself you were doing what you thought was best to escape your family's expectations. But the truth is, you left without even a backward glance because I didn't matter. My feelings didn't matter. You don't care about anyone or anything but yourself, do you?"

"Not true. So not true." Her voice was low and cool but she fluttered one hand over her stomach like he'd kicked her. Her dog, sensing the tension, seemed to get more excited, dancing around their feet.

"It is. I can't believe I've been so blind. I've been hanging on to this illusion of the girl you used to be in high school and college. But she has completely disappeared somewhere along the way."

"I'm sorry you had to read that."

"I won't let you and those bastards you work for get away with this," he growled. "No way in hell. I'll go to the media. To your family. To anybody who will listen."

"And say what? You have no proof of anything. Just leave it alone, Richard."

She was right. He was certain the incriminating document would be shredded and the memo purged from the NHC system the moment he walked out the door.

"You would love that, wouldn't you? If I just walked out and forgot everything. It's not going to happen. If I can't go to the media, I can at least do everything I can to protect your brother."

She took a deep breath. "That's not necessary."

His laugh was raw and scraped his throat. "Oh, believe me, Anna, as the hospital attorney and your brother's counsel now by default, I think it damn well is. Northeastern HealthCare is running out of time. I'm sure they're going to move fast. But we'll be ready for them."

He headed for the door but her voice stopped him.

"Richard, I... This is not what you think, I swear. Can you just give me a few days to straighten things out?"

"A few days? In a few days, your brother's life could be devastated. He's getting married in a week, Anna. Did you once think of that? A little accusation of sexual misconduct with a patient would be a hell of a thing to have hanging over his head on his honeymoon."

She drew in a shaky breath. "A few days. That's all I need."

"In a few days, this could be a done deal and your bloodsucking company could win. I am *not* going to let that happen."

She closed her eyes for a moment and the vulnerability on her features gave him the absurd urge to comfort her.

"Fine," she said after a moment. "Do what you have to do. And I will, too. Will you excuse me, then? I have a great deal of work to do."

Without another word, he spun on his heels and headed out the door.

He sat in his SUV for just a moment before turning the key in the ignition. Betrayal tasted like bitter ash in his mouth.

His mind flashed with images. Anna reading to Ethan

with his son snuggled against her and her features soft and affectionate. The way her eyes lit up when he kissed her. Making love with her and the tenderness that wrapped around them like a blanket on a cold winter's day…

All a mirage. He couldn't believe he was so stupid about her. So very, very blind.

He jerked the vehicle in gear and backed out of her driveway, hitting the speed dial on his cell phone as he went.

"Hi, Mom," he said when Diane answered. "I need you to keep Ethan a little longer, if you can."

"Is anything wrong, dear?"

What the hell wasn't wrong? He was in love with a woman willing to sacrifice her family for her career.

"Just a few work complications. I've got to run to the hospital. I'm sorry."

"No problem," his mother answered. "We're having a great time, aren't we, kiddo?"

He could hear Ethan giggling in the background and the pure sound of it centered him. He loved his son. He might feel like his legs had just been ripped out from underneath him but he still had Ethan, his mom, his practice. He had to hold on to the good things in his life. There would be time to mourn his shattered illusions later.

Right now, he needed to find Peter Wilder.

Any more shocks in her life and she was going to need a good cardiologist.

Anna sat numbly in her living room after Richard left. Lilli regarded her quizzically for a long moment then leapt onto her lap. Anna managed to yank herself out of her near-catatonia to pet the dog, while her mind continued to churn.

She felt like she was caught in the throes of a raging tornado for the past eighteen hours. The stunning news about her father, the outrageous discovery about NHC's plans for Walnut River General, making love with Richard and then being forced to face his bitter anger.

Lost somewhere in there had been his stunning declaration that he was in love with her.

I wouldn't want a little detail like the fact that I'm in love with you distract you from all that other important stuff in your life right now.

He couldn't be in love with her. Why would he possibly say such a thing? Still, she couldn't forget the emotion on his face the night before when he had held her, a certain light in his eyes as he kissed her.

I think you're a brilliant, capable, beautiful woman who doesn't see her own strengths. You don't see yourself as I do, as someone with the ability to cope with anything that comes along.

His words seemed etched in her memory, permanently imprinted there, just like the wild pulse of joy that had jumped inside her at his words, only to fade into shock a few moments later when he read that damn memo.

She buried her face in her hands. He couldn't love her. Not really. Obviously his feelings couldn't be very sure if he could tell her in one breath that he was in love with her, then believe her capable of betraying her own brother the next.

She remembered the disgust, the disillusionment in his eyes and wanted to weep. She could have told him everything, that she had just read the memo herself and was as sickened by it as he. The temptation to do just that had been overwhelming.

But she had known even as she opened her mouth that she couldn't do it. Richard had no legal access to an internal NHC memo, just as she had reminded him. But somehow she had a feeling that wouldn't have stopped him from taking on NHC and its powerhouse attorneys single-handedly and potentially endangering his own career.

She hadn't wanted him to take that risk. This was her mess and she was obligated to figure a way out of it herself. She wondered what Richard or her siblings would say if they knew she had been the one to bring Walnut General to the attention of her superiors at Northeastern HealthCare.

She had closed her eyes to some of the more questionable practices at NHC. Fury burned through her at her own negligence, her own gullibility. She should have known better. She should have remembered everything James Wilder tried to instill in his children. Things like character and strength and the awareness of greater good.

She had to fix this, and she had to do it on her own, no matter the cost to her job or her reputation.

She would probably face charges—or at least be sued. She had signed a nondisclosure clause when she took the job at NHC and whistle-blowing about an internal memo was in direct violation of what she had agreed to.

She was going to need a good attorney. Too bad she had just ensured the one man she trusted wanted nothing to do with her.

A sob welled up inside her but she choked it down. She had to keep it together. She had far too much to do right now to waste time sitting here feeling sorry for herself amid the wreckage of the life she had created for herself.

She picked up her cell phone and dialed Peter's number,

programmed there just like Ella's and David's, though she hadn't used any of them for months.

At first, she was frustrated when she was sent directly to voice mail, but then relief flooded her at the temporary reprieve.

Eventually she would have to explain to her older brother how stupid she had been, but at least for now she could escape with only leaving a message.

"Peter, it's Anna." Her voice trailed off as she floundered for words. "Look, this is going to sound really strange but I have a feeling Richard Green will be trying to get in touch with you. When you hear what he has to say, I would...ask you to withhold judgment for now. I have no right to ask you that. To ask you anything, really. But...I promise, I have my reasons. Just don't rush to conclusions, okay?"

She hung up, feeling even more like an idiot. Would he think she was crazy or would he give her a chance to explain?

She drew in a deep fortifying breath, then picked up her phone again. She had to fix this, no matter what might happen to her as a result. For her family's sake—and for her own—she had to make things right.

Chapter Twelve

Richard headed immediately to the hospital, where to his relief he found Peter Wilder's vehicle in his assigned parking space.

After checking Peter's office and the cafeteria, he finally found the man on the fourth floor in the administrative boardroom—along with Ella, David and J. D. Sumner.

Ella looked lovely and competent in surgical scrubs, her dark hair held away from her face with a headband, while her brothers and fiancé wore casual clothes, fitting for a Saturday.

Papers were scattered across the table and they all looked deep in conversation.

He hated what he was about to do to the Wilder family.

Not his fault, he reminded himself. He had done nothing. Anna and the bastards she worked for had created all of this. Acknowledging that didn't make his task any easier, though.

They were so engrossed in conversation that none of them noticed his presence for several moments until Peter finally looked up.

"Richard! Come in. Just the man we need to talk to."

"Oh?" He felt vaguely queasy at their eager smiles.

"We've decided we're not just tossing a white flag up in the air and giving in to Northeastern Health Care without a fight." Animation brightened Peter's features. "We need to come up with another plan for the municipal council to consider. A better alternative."

"Okay," he said slowly.

"What do you think of this? Walnut River wants out of the hospital business. Fine. I understand where they're coming from. With overhead and malpractice insurance costs through the roof, it's tough for public entities to stay viable in today's health-care market. We get it. But what if we could figure out a way to privatize the hospital without a takeover? If we could find local investors with the financial backing to purchase the hospital from the city?"

"That's a big *what if.*"

"Absolutely," David Wilder interjected. "But with just a few phone calls we've found several major players who are interested and I think we could get many of the local physicians to join up on a more limited basis."

"I really think we could make it work," Peter said. "This way the city would be out of the hospital business but decision-making control would still remain in local hands instead of some faceless corporate behemoth."

A corporate behemoth that intends to take you down. Richard forced a smile. "Sounds like you've thought it through."

"We're just in the beginning stages." Ella beamed with excitement. "But we need to know what legal hoops we'd have to jump through. That's where you come in."

All three of the Wilders were humming with energy and he hated even more what he had to tell them about their sister. He, conversely, was suddenly exhausted. At the same time, he was filled with a fierce desire to do everything he possibly could to beat Northeastern Health-Care any freaking way possible.

"I'm in," he said promptly. "Whatever you need, I'll help you."

It was the least he could do, especially since they would soon be dealing with Anna's latest betrayal.

"I knew you would help us."

Ella smiled at him and for the first time Richard saw a trace of Anna in her smile. How had he missed the resemblance all these years? Was it simply because he had been acting on the assumption that Anna was adopted and hadn't been looking for it?

What else had he missed about Anna Wilder? he wondered.

"So what brings you here on a Saturday afternoon? Was there something you needed?" Peter asked.

Richard could feel his shoulders tense and he forced himself to relax as much as possible. "I need to speak with you," he finally said. "It's about Anna."

"What about her?" Ella asked, and Richard didn't miss her sudden tension or the disgust dragging down the corners of David's mouth or Peter's weary resignation. Only J.D. looked impartial, but Richard was quite confident that would quickly change.

"Perhaps this would be better in private."

"He'll only tell us what you said after you leave," Ella said.

"Not necessarily," Peter murmured, exchanging a look with Richard.

"You can use my office if you need a place to talk," J.D. offered.

"Thanks," Richard said, then led the way down the hall to the administrator's office.

"What's going on?" Peter asked when Richard closed the door behind the two of them.

Richard let out a long weary breath. This was a miserable thing to have to dump on a man as conscientious and upright as Peter Wilder. "I hate to be the one to tell you this, but you need to know what Northeastern Health-Care is planning."

He briefly outlined the memo he had inadvertently read, including their underhanded strategy to defeat the opposition by taking Peter out through any means necessary.

When he finished, Peter's features were taut with fury. "Sexual misconduct allegations? Malpractice?"

He paused and seemed at a loss for words. "What the hell kind of people does Anna work with?" he finally said.

"We knew they would fight hard and possibly fight dirty to obtain such a potentially lucrative hospital."

"Yes, but I never expected something so underhanded. And you're telling me Anna knew about the memo? About what they planned?"

He hated every moment of this. "I'm sorry. I found it at her place. She told me to stay out of it. That it wasn't any of my business."

Peter raked a hand through his hair, his eyes dark with betrayal. "She called while I was talking to a potential investor earlier but I haven't had time to check my messages."

"I have no proof, Pete. Only what I saw. I couldn't take it from her house since I didn't have any legal right to access the corporation's internal documents. It would have been theft."

"Even if it was there in plain sight?"

"It wasn't. Not really. I wouldn't have even seen it except some papers fell when we were…" Fighting. Kissing. What the hell difference did it make? He caught himself just in time from offering either answer. "When we were talking. I went to pick them up and saw the memo."

"My own sister is willing to throw me to the wolves. How could she be a party to such a thing?"

"I can't answer that," Richard answered.

"I thought after last night, maybe we could manage to salvage some relationship with her. Things seemed… different with her after she read the letter."

"I'm sorry." It was painfully inadequate but he had nothing else to offer.

"This is going to kill Ella. As angry as she's been at Anna, she still misses her sister, especially with all the weddings coming up in the family."

"You have to tell them."

Peter nodded, not looking at all thrilled at the prospect. "If we have no proof of what they're planning, how can we fight it?"

"You're getting married in a week. Any chance you might be willing to take a little personal time, reschedule your appointments, to stay away from the hospital? If you're not seeing patients, they can't entrap you, either through malpractice allegations or anything else."

"I'm not running and hiding! That's not the way my father would handle this and it's not the way I will, either."

He expected exactly that answer. Richard sighed. "I have a few other ideas. None of them easy."

"I don't care," Peter snapped. "I am not going to let them win, no matter what it takes."

Saturday afternoon at Walnut River General brought back a world of memories for Anna: the light slanting through the front doors, the smell inside of cafeteria food, the underlying hint of antiseptic and antibiotics, and the slightly quieter pace.

How many Saturdays of her youth had been spent here waiting for her father while he wrapped up just one more bit of paperwork or attended to one more patient?

Her memories seemed so rich and fresh as she stood in the lobby that she almost expected him to come striding through the halls of the hospital, his stethoscope around his neck, his white coat flapping behind him and that steely determination in his blue eyes.

Oh, she missed her father.

The last eight years had been so strained between them that she couldn't think of him at all without this hollow ache of regret inside her. So much wasted time. She would have given anything if her father had once communicated in person the things he'd written in that letter about being proud of her and supporting her career choices.

Instead, she had always felt the bitter sting of knowing she had disappointed him.

She pushed the familiar pain away and approached the security guard seated behind the information desk.

"I'm looking for my brother, Dr. Peter Wilder. He

wasn't at home and his car is parked in his parking space out front. Can you give me some idea where I might be able to find him?"

"Don't know. Sorry."

His expression was cool, bordering on hostile, and she sighed. She had never met this man in her life. The only reason she could think for his pugnacity was that he belonged to the anti-merger camp and knew she worked for NHC.

She didn't have time to play hospital politics. Not today.

"Would you page him for me, then?" she asked briskly.

He went on reading his newspaper as if he hadn't heard her and she nearly growled with frustration.

"It's important," she finally said. "A family emergency."

Though he hesitated, she could see the wheels in his head turning as he wondered whether he might be incurring Peter's wrath by delaying. Finally he picked up the phone and punched in Peter's pager number.

She drummed her fingers on the counter, impatient for her brother to return the page. She was still waiting a few moments later when the elevator doors opened and the absolute last person she wanted to see right now—okay, last five, at least—walked out.

Ella's eyes were swollen and her nose was red, as if she had been crying. Anna had just a moment's advantage since Ella was busy digging through the messenger bag slung diagonally over her shoulder and didn't see her immediately.

Her sister pulled out her cell phone and started to punch in a number when her gaze suddenly caught sight of Anna and her fingers froze on the phone.

Anna was grateful for the tiny window of opportunity

she'd had to prepare herself for the coming confrontation. Otherwise, she was certain Ella's vicious stare would have destroyed her on the spot.

In some corner of her mind, she knew her imagination was running in overdrive but suddenly the previously empty foyer seemed filled with people, all of their attention focused on the two sisters.

Every warning bell inside her was clanging, warning her to escape, that she didn't need this right now. But she couldn't do it. Though it was one of the hardest things she'd ever done, she forced herself to step forward, until she was only a few feet away.

"Ella," she murmured, aching inside, wishing she could make everything right again. After that one word, she had no idea what else to say, but her sister didn't give her a chance, anyway.

Ella glared at her. "If we were kids again, I'd be ripping your hair out right now. Literally. Hank by painful hank, until your eyes watered so much you couldn't see."

Under less dire circumstances, Anna might have smiled at the threat and the way Ella's hands fisted on her messenger bag. She wouldn't have put anything past her feisty little sister. Ella might have been the youngest Wilder but she had always been able to hold her own with the rest of them.

Suddenly Anna missed her sister and the closeness they had once shared, with a fierce hollow yearning. She missed late-night gab sessions and shopping trips to the mall and fighting over their shared bathroom.

While Anna was trying so hard to prove herself, her sister had become a beautiful dedicated physician and she had missed the whole process because of her foolishness.

"Don't believe everything you hear, El."

"Are you calling Richard Green a liar? He knows what he saw in that memo and I believe every word he says."

Anna closed her eyes, hurt all over again that Richard had so quickly allied himself with her siblings against her, that he trusted her integrity so little.

With good reason, she reminded herself. She couldn't blame him for this. She had created the mess through her own stupidity and it was up to her to make it right.

The magnitude of the task ahead of her seemed daunting, terrifying, but she had to do it, for her family's sake and for her own.

"I would never call Richard a liar. He saw exactly what he said he saw."

"So you admit it!" If anything, the shadows under Ella's eyes looked darker, almost bruised. "You're part of Northeastern HealthCare's dirty tactics to destroy Peter's reputation! How could you, Anna?"

"I didn't know about the memo, El."

"That's easy to say now that we know about it."

She couldn't argue with Ella. Nothing she said would convince her sister, and in the meantime, she was wasting valuable time.

"I'm not going to stand here in the hospital foyer and have a shouting match with you. You'll believe what you want to believe. Nothing I say will make any difference."

Ella's mouth drooped and she looked as if she might cry again. "What happened to you, Anna? The sister I loved so much would never have been a party to something like this."

Ella's use of the past tense sent a shaft of pain through her but Anna fought it down. She deserved all of this. How could she blame Ella for thinking the worst of her when she had purposely created so much distance between them that Ella had nothing else to judge her by?

"Can you tell me where to find Peter?"

"Why? Have you come to twist the knife a little harder?"

She sighed. "Where is he, El?"

She thought for a moment her sister wasn't going to answer but then she shrugged. "He's in his office with Richard. They're working on strategy."

Great. Not only did she have to face her livid brother but now she had to see Richard again. This was shaping up to be one fabulous day.

"None of us will let you do this to him, Anna," Ella said, her voice fierce and determined. "You need to know that. Whatever friends Northeastern HealthCare has in this hospital won't be on your side for long when word leaks out about these dirty tactics. The entire hospital will mobilize to protect Peter before we let you destroy him."

"Fair enough," Anna murmured.

Knowing any further arguments with Ella were futile and would only deepen the chasm between them, she turned away and headed for the elevator.

As she rode up to the fourth floor, she realized Peter had kept his part of the bargain from the night before. She was certain of it. He was still leaving the choice of telling David and Ella about their father's letter up to Anna. If she had learned about James's indiscretion that had resulted in Anna's conception, Ella would have said something. She would have at least looked at her a little differently.

The last thing any of them probably wanted right now was a closer kinship with her.

The door to Peter's office suite was closed and her hands trembled as she reached to open it.

Forget this and go home.

The thought whispered through her mind and for an instant, she was deeply tempted. Seeing the disillusionment in her brother's eyes would be hard enough. Seeing it all over again in Richard's and knowing she had lost his love forever would be unbearable.

She stood for a long moment, trying to bolster her courage. She had no idea what she would say to Peter but she had to attempt some kind of explanation.

Finally she knocked on the door before she could talk herself out of it.

"Yeah," Peter said gruffly and she took that as all the invitation she was likely to receive.

She pushed the door open and nearly wept with relief to find her brother alone in his office.

"Where's Richard? Ella said he was up here with you." It was the first thing she could think of to say but Peter didn't seem to think it was an odd opening volley.

"He had to leave to pick up Ethan. His son."

"I know who Ethan is. He's a great kid."

She was stalling. She recognized it but this was so excruciatingly hard with Peter watching her out of those eyes that reminded her so much of their father's.

"I guess you're probably surprised to see me."

He shrugged. "I wouldn't have expected you to show your face around here right about now. It's a good thing David had to meet Courtney and Janie downtown or you wouldn't have made it this far."

She laughed bitterly. "Ella threatened to yank my hair out down in the lobby."

"What did you expect?"

The hard edge to his expression made her want to flee but she hardened her resolve and clasped her hands together in her lap.

"I didn't know about the memo, Peter. I swear I didn't. I know you have no reason to believe me, but it's the truth. I found it just minutes before Richard arrived. It was top secret and on a private server I shouldn't have had access to, but my boss gave me his password to upload some documents regarding the merger and it was just…there. I made a backup copy of it for my files and printed it out and was trying to figure out what to do when Richard showed up and saw it."

He was quiet for a long moment, studying her features intently. "And what did you decide to do?" he finally asked, his voice so controlled she couldn't begin to guess whether he believed her or not.

She lifted her chin. "I'm a Wilder. Of course I'm going to do the right thing!"

He smiled with such sudden brilliance she felt a little lightheaded. "Of course you're going to do the right thing."

His certainty washed through her, warm and soothing. He believed her. The rest of the world might think she was a sleazy, sneaky corporate mole but Peter believed her.

To her chagrin, her eyes burned with emotion and a single tear escaped to trickle down her face.

"I'm sorry. I just…I thought you would be as convinced as everyone else that I intended all this from the start."

Peter stepped forward and pulled her into a quick hug. "Richard put forward a convincing argument. But some part of me still couldn't quite believe it."

She leaned against him for only a moment while she struggled to regain her composure.

"I've been a fool. There were other warning signs of NHC's more questionable business practices among the top level of brass but I ignored them. My other boss is a good decent man, so I convinced myself I was imagining things. I was on the fast track there and I convinced myself they were harmless and that I could make a difference when I moved up in management. I never expected these sorts of underhanded tactics, especially not against my own brother. I should have, though. If they make good on any of the strategies outlined in the memo, I'll never forgive myself."

"We're not going to let them get away with it, Anna."

"Neither am I," she said grimly. "It's going to take me some time, though. For a few days, it may seem as if things are continuing normally with the merger negotiations and the board vote Thursday. I know I've given you absolutely no reason, but I have to ask you to trust me, just for a few days."

"Okay."

Just like that.

His faith made her want to weep again but she drew herself together. "In the meantime, listen to Richard. He can help you protect yourself against whatever Alfred Daly and his cohorts might have up their sleeves."

"He wants me to take this week off before the wedding."

"Not a bad idea."

"I won't run. Dad wouldn't have."

She smiled, sensing a ray of light for the first time since she opened that file on Daly's server earlier that day. "No, he wouldn't have."

"You're more like him than you've ever given yourself credit for," Peter said.

"Not yet," she answered with a shaky smile. "But I'm getting there."

Chapter Thirteen

"Hurry up or we're going to be late, Ethan. Where's your baseball glove?"

"Don't know." His son remained remarkably unconcerned that his last T-ball game was supposed to start in forty-five minutes as he continued playing with his Matchbox cars.

Richard drew in a deep breath. Trying for patience was just about the toughest task he faced as a father—especially since Ethan was easily distracted and usually bubbled over with energy.

The process of encouraging him to stay on task was tougher than facing a whole courtroom full of high-powered attorneys.

"Think. Where did you have it last?"

Ethan zoomed one of his trucks along the edge of the carpet where it met the hardwood flooring. "Outside, I guess. Me and Grandma played catch earlier today. I think maybe I left it there."

"So go look for it, or we're not going to make it to your game."

His snappish tone finally captured Ethan's attention. He dropped his car and gave his father a wounded look. "We have to go! It's my last game!"

"Then go find your glove."

Ethan glared at him but headed for the backyard in search of the missing equipment, leaving Richard with only his guilt for company.

He needed to practice a little more patience with his son. His bad mood wasn't Ethan's fault. Richard knew exactly why he had been irritable and out of sorts for the past four days.

Anna Wilder.

He hadn't seen her since Saturday morning at her duplex but she hadn't been far from his thoughts. He had done his best to push away the memory of making love to her but sometimes random images intruded into his mind, usually at the most inopportune moment.

Despite that little glitch, for the most part his whole world had condensed to two clear objectives—protecting Peter Wilder and beating the hell out of NHC in the merger negotiations. Everything he did was aimed at those goals.

So far, Peter appeared to be safe. No malpractice allegations or harassment claims had emerged out of the woodwork. Since the hospital board vote was scheduled for first thing in the morning, he had to look at the relative quiet as a positive indicator that NHC had reconsidered the strategies outlined in that damn memo.

He wasn't letting down his guard, though, and he wasn't allowing Peter to do so, either. He had been fiercely busy wrapping Anna's brother in as many legal safeguards as he could devise.

To his further frustration, Peter seemed remarkably unconcerned about any possible threat to his reputation or his practice, until Richard wanted to shake him out of his complacency.

"See, Dad? I found it! I told you it was in the backyard."

Ethan still looked annoyed at him for the flare of temper so Richard forced himself to smile. "Good job. We'd better get going."

On the way out to the SUV, he closed his eyes and arched his neck one way and then the other, trying to force his shoulders to relax. He couldn't take his grim mood out on his son. Ethan didn't deserve it. The one person who did deserve it was making herself remarkably scarce.

Ethan jabbered all the way to the park where he played T-ball. When they were a few blocks from the baseball field, he suddenly stopped in the middle of a soliloquy about the playdate he had enjoyed with a friend that afternoon.

"Hey, Dad, Anna said she would come to another one of my games. She promised, remember, the night she read me the funny story about the worm and the spider? This is my last one. Do you think she'll be there?"

Apparently, Richard wasn't the only one who couldn't stop thinking about a certain lovely blond double-crosser.

"Anna's really busy right now," he murmured. *Destroying the hospital her father dedicated his life to, and her family in the process.* "She might not make it."

"She promised," Ethan said, his voice brimming with

confidence. "I wonder if she'll bring Lilli. Do you think she'll let me walk her again? I sure like that dog."

He so hated that his son had to learn the lesson early in life that some people couldn't be trusted to remember things like honor and decency and promises made. He wanted Ethan to hang on to his illusions for a little bit longer.

"We'll have to see what happens. Like I said, Anna is really busy right now."

But to his shock, when they arrived at the ball diamond, she was the first person he saw. She sat on the top bench of the bleachers, looking sleek and elegant even in Levi's and a crisp white shirt.

At the sight of her, his heart gave a slow surge of welcome and his body tightened with longing. How was it that when he was away from her, he always managed to forget how her long blond loveliness took his breath away?

"She's here! I knew she would come. Do you see her, Dad?"

"I see her," he answered, his voice gruff. Fast on the heels of his initial pleasure at seeing her was hot hard anger that racketed through him like a pinball.

Why the hell couldn't she leave him alone? This was hard enough for him, knowing how stupid he had been for her.

Even knowing what she was, what she was part of, he couldn't keep himself from wanting her.

"I'm gonna show her how good I am at catching the ball now." Ethan raced ahead of him and climbed like a little howler monkey up the bleachers to talk to Anna. Richard was grateful for the few minutes to gain control of the wild surge of emotions. By the time he reached them, the careening emotions inside him had faded to a dull ache instead of that terrible, piercing pain.

Her blue eyes held wariness and something else—something elusive and tantalizing that he couldn't quite identify.

"Hi." She pitched her voice low.

He nodded, but didn't quite trust himself not to yell at her all over again so he said nothing.

"I promised I would be here," she said. "I didn't want to let Ethan down."

She was willing to crucify her own brother but she didn't want to break a promise to a five-year-old boy? He gave her a skeptical look and she had the grace to flush.

"Where's Lilli?" Ethan asked. "Did you bring her?"

"Not tonight. She hasn't been feeling good the last couple of days. I think she has a cold."

"Dogs get colds?"

"Sometimes. Or maybe it's just allergies."

He looked disappointed for about half a second, then with rapid-fire speed, his mood cycled back to excitement. "Hey, guess what, Anna? Me and my grandma played catch all day today and now I'm super good. I won't miss another fly ball, ever again. Wanna see?"

"Absolutely. Bring it on."

She gripped Ethan's hand and climbed down from the bleachers, smiling at his son with such genuine pleasure that Richard felt as if his heart were being ripped into tiny pieces.

Ethan grinned back and shoved the ball at Richard. "Dad, can you throw it at me so I can show Anna how good I catch?"

"Sure. Let's step away from the bleachers a little so we don't hit anybody if we miss the ball."

"I'm not going to miss, Dad. I told you, I've been practicing."

"It's not you I'm worried about, it's me. I don't even have a glove."

"I won't throw hard, okay?"

Still doing his best not to look at her, he led Ethan to an open stretch of ground between two playing fields. He tossed the ball to his son and was pleased when Ethan easily caught it in his glove.

"Good job!" Anna exclaimed. "You have been practicing."

"Yep. Now watch me throw it back!" He tossed it back to Richard, harder than he expected and a little to the right. Richard managed to snag it with his bare hands, but it was a near thing.

Anna stood watching them both play catch for several minutes, her features revealing little of her thoughts, until Ethan's coach blew a whistle to call his team into the dugout.

Ethan ran off eagerly, leaving Richard alone with her—exactly the position he didn't want to find himself.

They made their way back toward the bleachers in silence. Just before they reached them, Anna touched the bare skin of his forearm to stop him. She dropped her hand quickly but not before the heat of her fingers scorched through him.

"I'm sorry. I'm sure you're wishing me to Hades right about now. But I did promise Ethan."

"I wouldn't want you to break a promise."

That delicate flush coated her cheekbones and he wondered at it. How could she possibly still have the ability to blush?

"Have you talked to Peter?" she asked after a moment.

"Several times. He seems remarkably nonchalant for a man whose sister is trying to destroy him."

"Has anything…happened?"

"You tell me. You're the one with all the inside information."

Her jaw clenched at his bitter tone. "You're going to believe what you want to believe."

"No. I'm going to believe the evidence. I'm an attorney. That's what we do."

"Maybe the evidence isn't as cut-and-dried as you think."

He opened his mouth to offer a scathing rebuke but she cut him off with a shake of her head.

"I didn't come here to fight with you, Richard. I also didn't want to spoil the game for you. I'll just watch an inning or two and then get out of your way. You'll hardly know I'm here."

He was saved from having to respond by Ethan's team taking the field.

The park had two sets of bleachers and she at least had the courtesy to sit on the other bleachers, several dozen feet away from him. That didn't stop his gaze from drifting in her direction entirely too often.

He knew it was crazy but he could almost smell her from here, that feminine, sexy scent of hers.

He didn't miss the way she stood up and cheered when Ethan caught a fly ball to end the inning half and then again a few minutes later when his son hit a two-run single. When his son crossed home plate, sent home by another player's hit, Richard also didn't miss the way Ethan grinned triumphantly first at his father then turned to aim the same grin at Anna.

Damn her. His heart was already shattered. Did she have to do the same thing to his son's?

She lasted all of an inning and a half—long enough to watch Ethan hit another single—before she couldn't bear another minute.

As she slid down the bleachers, the sun was just dipping below the horizon, bathing the baseball diamond in the pale rosy light of dusk. She closed her eyes, wanting to store up this moment.

It had been foolish to come. Foolish and self-indulgent. She had hoped four days of reflection would have had some kind of impact on Richard, that perhaps he might begin to experience a little doubt about her guilt.

She supposed some optimistic corner of her heart had hoped he'd begun to wonder if he might have been wrong about her.

Obviously, that hadn't happened. He was as angry as he had been Saturday morning when he had seen that memo. More so, maybe. Hearing the bitterness in his voice, seeing the cold disdain in those eyes that had once looked at her with such warm tenderness, had been chilling proof that nothing had changed.

She walked back to her car with one hand curled against the crushing pain in her chest.

Nothing had changed and everything had changed. The wheels she had set in motion couldn't be stopped now.

Now she just had to wait and see what happened.

* * *

Richard walked into the hospital the next morning in his best suit and his favorite power tie. He had slept little the night before. After tossing and turning for a couple of hours, he had finally risen well before dawn.

He wanted to think it was diligence to his client that kept him up and not his last glimpse of Anna as she had left the baseball diamond. Unfortunately, he knew otherwise.

He was totally committed to representing the hospital to the best of his ability but the images haunting his fragmented dreams hadn't had anything to do with the hospital. They had everything to do with Anna.

He wanted this hospital board meeting to be over. Though the merger vote was still too close to call, at this point he just wanted a damn decision. Then maybe this sense of impending doom would dissipate. At least Peter would be safe—and maybe Anna would return to New York where she belonged and he wouldn't have to spend a sleepless night every time he happened to bump into her.

He would probably see her this morning at the board meeting. Twisted as he was, he couldn't help the little buzz of anticipation at the prospect.

He sighed as he walked through the lobby. The security guard waved and grinned at him. Richard managed a half-hearted wave, then furrowed his brow when three more staff members beamed at him on his way to the elevator.

Weird.

Though he usually didn't buy into those woo-woo kind of things, he sensed a curious energy in the air. The impression was reinforced when he rode the elevator with Bob Barrett, a physician he knew only casually. The man actually patted him on the back when the elevator stopped at the second floor.

"It's a great day for Walnut River General, isn't it?" he said, before stepping out.

Something definitely odd was going on. He couldn't begin to figure out what.

The first person he met coming out of the elevator on the administrative floor was Ella Wilder. She aimed a thousand-watt smile at him, then went one better, throwing her arms around him.

"Isn't it wonderful?" she exclaimed. "The best news I can imagine. Peter and Bethany's wedding this weekend will truly be a celebration."

Before he could ask her what the hell she was talking about, she released him and jumped into the waiting elevator just before the doors closed, leaving him completely befuddled.

He headed to J.D.'s office, hoping Ella's fiancé could shed a little light on things.

J.D. wasn't alone. Peter Wilder stood in the outer office with him and his assistant, Tina Tremaine, and all of them looked jubilant.

"I knew she would come through for us," Peter exulted when he saw Richard. "She's a Wilder, isn't she?"

He frowned. "Who? Ella?"

"Of course not. Anna!" He grinned at Richard but his smile faded when he took in his confusion. "I'm guessing you haven't read the paper this morning."

"I didn't have a chance. I was too busy prepping for this morning's board meeting." And brooding about Peter's sister. "Why? What did I miss?"

J.D. and Peter exchanged laughing looks. "Maybe

you'd better come into my office and see for yourself," J.D. said. "My staff made sure I received a copy."

He opened the door behind him and Richard was stunned to see every available surface covered with the front page of the *Walnut River Courier.*

The same headline in huge type screamed from all of them: Northeastern HealthCare Drops Hospital Bid.

A subhead read: Municipal Council Considering Options, May Look to Private Investors.

He stared at the headline and then at both men. "They're pulling out? After six months of fighting? Just like that?"

Peter laughed. "No. Not just like that. My brilliant baby sister did it all. In five days, she managed to accomplish what the rest of us have been trying to pull off for months."

He shook his head to clear the fuzziness out, wishing all over again that he'd been able to grab more than a few hours of restless sleep. He grabbed one of the newspapers off the wall and read the first few paragraphs, stopping when he reached the statement released by NHC.

He read,

Upon further study, we have determined that Walnut River General would not be a good fit for NHC. We regret that we will not have the opportunity to bring our winning health-care model to the citizens of Walnut River but wish the community and hospital personnel all the best.

It was definitely a blow-off quote, leaving NHC very little room to reconsider.

"I'm sorry. I'm lost here. You're going to have to back up a step or two for me. What is this? Why did they pull out? And why do you seem to think Anna had anything to do with it? Last I heard, she was the enemy. What about the infamous memo?"

"That memo is the best thing that's ever happened to the merger opposition," J.D. answered.

"How can that be possible?" he growled.

"Because finding it infuriated Anna and mobilized her to our side," Peter answered.

"What do you mean, finding it? She knew about it all along."

Peter shook his head. "No, she didn't."

"So she says." He couldn't keep the bitterness out of his voice, the deep sense of betrayal.

Peter frowned and gestured to the newspaper headlines blaring across the room. "This is evidence she's telling the truth. Do you really think NHC would have dropped their bid for the hospital if Anna hadn't maneuvered things so they had no other choice?"

"How?"

"She's brilliant," J.D. said. "Savvy and smart. She single-handedly orchestrated what amounts to an internal coup to force them out."

"She knew there was an anti-Daly faction at NHC, shareholders and other top-level executives who weren't happy with some of his tactics," Peter added. "Anna has been working like a demon for the last four days, negotiating with them. She agreed to deliver the memo as evidence against Daly to force him out if they would consent to drop their bid for the hospital. It all hit the fan yesterday. Daly's out at Northeastern HealthCare, a new guard is in and their first action was to issue the statement withdrawing their bid for the hospital, as promised."

Richard felt as if J.D. and Peter had both taken turns pummeling him with an office chair.

He tried to remember Anna's demeanor Saturday morning when he read the memo at her apartment. She had been shaky and uneasy, he remembered. Pale, nervous, edgy. But he had just attributed it to guilt that he had found out about NHC's nefarious plans for Peter.

Was it possible she hadn't known? When she had faced all his accusations, could she have been withholding evidence that would have exonerated her?

He couldn't seem to wrap his head around it. He had been hard, bordering on cruel. *You're a cold heartless woman who is willing to sell your own family down the river to get your way.*

Those had been his words. And she had stood there absorbing them. Why the hell hadn't she tried to defend herself? She had stood there and let him rip into her without saying a thing.

Not quite true, he remembered with growing self-disgust. She had told him he was jumping to unfounded conclusions. She had asked him to give her a few days to straighten things out but he had assumed she was only trying to delay him from taking action until after the vote.

Just last night, she had told him that maybe the evidence wasn't as cut-and-dried as he wanted to believe.

She had skirted the truth but hadn't told him all of it.

She hadn't trusted him. That's what it all came down to. She had taken his criticism without explaining anything at all of substance to him.

And he deserved her lack of trust. He had jumped to conclusions, had based his entire perceptions of her guilt and innocence on past misdeeds that should have been inadmissible.

Because of what happened eight years before, he had been completely unwilling to give her any benefit of doubt. When he saw that memo, he had taken it as damning evidence against her—proof of her perfidy, he now realized, that he had been looking for all along.

Even if she had tried to defend herself a little more strenuously, he wasn't sure he would have allowed himself to believe her.

He had told her he loved her.

It hadn't been a lie, exactly. He did love her. But love without trust was flimsy and hollow.

"So obviously the board vote this morning has been canceled," Peter interrupted his thoughts. "We're moving ahead with our efforts to privatize the hospital. Is your firm still willing to help us through the legalities?"

"Of course," he answered absently.

"Excellent," J.D. said. "We'd like you to draw up a preliminary partnership agreement as soon as possible so we can present it to the city council. I know this is an imposition, but can you work up a rough draft today?"

"No problem. I allocated most of the day to hospital business, with the merger vote and possible follow-up work. I can have it to you by this afternoon."

"Thanks, Richard," Peter said. "I knew we could count on you."

The other man's words scraped his conscience raw. Anna should have been able to count on him, on the man who claimed he loved her. He should have trusted his own heart, not a stupid piece of paper. Instead, Richard had rushed to convict her without any kind of trial.

He would be lucky if she ever wanted to see him again.

Chapter Fourteen

"We're serious about this, Anna. We want you to stay."

Anna watched Lilli chase her favorite toy, wondering why she couldn't manage to drum up a little more enthusiasm for Wallace Jeffers's unbelievable offer. He wanted her to take over his position as vice president of the mergers and acquisitions division of NHC since he was poised to move into Alfred Daly's newly vacated spot.

This was what she had dreamed about for eight years. Wallace had been her mentor at NHC, the reason she had taken the job there in the first place. He had been one of those at the company who predicted a great future for her there and now that he was taking over for Daly, he appeared to be willing to make those predictions reality.

She should be over the moon. She should be doing cartwheels, sending notice to all the trade papers, ordering new business cards.

Instead, she sat in her rented duplex, watching her dog drool all over a rubber lizard and trying to summon a little excitement. "I appreciate your trust in me, Wallace. I do. But I'm going to have to think about this."

"What's to think about?" He sounded genuinely startled. "It's a no-brainer, Anna. If you take this job, you'll be completely skipping over several rungs in the corporate ladder."

"I know that. It's an incredible offer and I'm grateful. I just need a little time to think about it."

"We need to move fast to reorganize the company if we want to enact the kind of changes some of us have been pushing for a long time. I'm going to need an answer sooner rather than later."

"Can I at least have a few hours?"

She had been thinking for five days that she was going to lose her job and now she was being offered the promotion of her dreams. It was enough to make her head spin.

He sighed. "I want you on board, Anna. Without you having the guts to come forward with that memo we used to push Daly out, none of this would have happened. I want people of integrity and grit on my team. You've earned this promotion. No one in that department works harder than you do or gets my vision more clearly."

She had nothing but respect for Wallace Jeffers and knew that under his leadership, NHC would thrive. She was deeply flattered that he had enough faith in her to believe her capable of replacing him. She ought to just say yes right now and start packing her bags to return to New York, but the words seemed to clog in her throat.

"I appreciate your offer. I'm just…I have to consider my options right now."

"What options?" His voice sharpened. "Have you got another offer I don't know about?"

"No," she assured him. "Nothing like that."

"Then what?"

My heart is here.

She couldn't say the words, not to her boss, a man she respected professionally and personally.

"Give me a few hours, Wallace. I'll call you back by the end of the day, I promise."

"All right. Just make sure you give yourself enough time to pack up and be back here for an 8 a.m. staff meeting so I can introduce the new leadership team of Northeastern HealthCare."

She managed a laugh. "You're so confident I'll say yes?"

"You'd be stupid not to take this promotion, and you are far from a stupid woman, Anna."

Wrong, she thought sadly. She was stupid. A smart woman would walk away from Walnut River and not look back. But these past few weeks had shown her how deeply her life and the person she had become were intertwined with this community and the people who lived here.

She wasn't sure she was ready to leave.

What was her alternative, though? Jobs in her field weren't exactly thick on the ground in Walnut River. And even if she found one, what would she gain by staying? Only more heartache, she was certain.

She sighed. Why delay the inevitable? She couldn't turn down Wallace's offer. She should just pick up the phone right now and tell him yes. What did Walnut River have to offer her?

She even picked up her cell phone, nerves strumming

through her, but Lilli suddenly barked with excitement and raced to the door and Anna's hand froze on the numbers.

Richard?

Her heart jumped along with her little dog as the doorbell rang.

It wouldn't be, she told herself, though she couldn't help the little spasm of hope that faded when she opened the door. Instead of Richard Green, she was instantly assaulted by her entire family. Peter, David, Ella and their significant others—Bethany Holloway, J. D. Sumner and a lovely brown-eyed blonde she assumed was David's fiancée, Courtney Albright.

"There's my baby sister," David announced before she could even greet them.

She opened her mouth to answer but the words were snatched away when he scooped her into his arms and twirled her around her miniscule living room until her head spun while Lilli yipped and danced around their ankles.

"David," she exclaimed. "Put me down before you either step on my dog or make me puke."

"You're still motion sick? I would have thought you outgrew that years ago."

"Not completely," she said as her stomach churned.

"Ew," he said, releasing her so abruptly she almost fell.

Peter was there to catch her, though. Before she could even find her breath, he pulled her into his arms, enveloping her in a tight hug.

"You didn't let us down, Anna."

His voice sounded so much like their father's. "I knew you could do it. If anyone could save Walnut River General Hospital, I knew it would be you. You were amazing. Absolutely amazing."

She allowed herself one quick moment to bask in the warm glow of her siblings' approval before she pulled away. She had to tell them the truth, the one she had been withholding from them for months.

"You know my company wouldn't have even looked at Walnut River General if not for me, don't you? I'm the one who proposed the hospital as a possible acquisition target in the first place."

Peter made a face. "Okay, so you're not completely perfect. But we're still keeping you."

She almost cried then, holding her tears in by sheer force of will as Peter gave her another tight hug then released her.

"My turn," Ella said, stepping forward.

Anna stared at her little sister, overwhelmed, for just a second too long. Ella's expression started to cool, her arms to drop, and Anna's tears broke free.

"El," she murmured, just that, then grabbed her sister tightly.

For so long she had lived with a hole in her heart without even realizing it. She had tried to fill it with work, never realizing it would always be empty until she made her peace with her family.

Now she stood and rocked with her arms around her sister, the tears trickling down her cheeks.

"I have missed you so much," Ella said.

"I'm sorry. I'm so sorry."

"No. I'm the one who's sorry. I said awful things to you."

"I deserved them. All of them. I've been so stupid. Incredibly stupid. When I dropped out of med school, I was sure I had failed everyone. I thought I had to choose between my career and my family. If I wasn't in medicine, I felt like I didn't belong with the rest of you."

"You do," Ella exclaimed. "Of course you do. You always have."

Anna saw that now. She was a Wilder. It didn't matter whether she was their half sister or their adopted sister. Either way, she belonged in this family. She loved them and needed them in her life and she had been so very foolish to believe she could take on the world by herself.

"You're our sister and we love you," Ella said. "We have all missed you."

"Oh, Ella." She sniffled again.

Sometime soon she would tell Ella and David about the letter from their father but not today, she decided.

"Cut it out, you two," David interrupted. "This is supposed to be a party. A celebration of good triumphing over evil. No offense, Anna."

She couldn't help but laugh. "Oh, none taken, I'm sure."

"We even have champagne," Bethany interjected.

"And food," the other woman added. "Hi. I'm Courtney. I'm thrilled to finally meet you. You have to come to dinner sometime soon so you can meet my little girl, Janie. She's thrilled at the prospect of another aunt to add to her growing family."

To Anna's surprise, David's fiancée gave her a warm hug, as did Bethany and even J.D.

"You can't get away from them all now," J.D. murmured in her ear. "You Wilders are relentless. You had your chance to escape but now you're stuck."

Anna had been alone for so long that the prospect of all this family was daunting but wonderful at the same time.

She looked around at her siblings and their loved ones and she had to laugh. "I just have one question. If you're all here, who's left to run the hospital?"

"Nobody. We closed down so we could come and celebrate with you," David deadpanned.

"I've actually got to go back on in an hour," Ella said. "So I'm afraid I'll have to skip the champagne."

"Ha. I'm off rotation for five whole days," David boasted.

"Lucky," Ella muttered.

"Just wait. When you're an attending, you'll be able to flaunt it over all the lowly residents, too," he said with a grin.

Anna smiled at their banter. Once she would have felt excluded when the rest of the Wilders talked shop. It used to bug the heck out of her and she would always bite down frustration when family discussions inevitably turned to medicine. Now she realized her annoyance had been a result of her own insecurities.

If she hadn't wanted to talk medicine, all she would have had to do was change the subject instead of simmering in her separateness.

"Bring on the champagne," Peter said, distracting her from her thoughts.

"I'm afraid I don't have enough glasses."

"No problem." Bethany grinned. "We brought our own. Courtney thought of everything."

Out of a wicker basket, they pulled out plastic champagne flutes along with cheese, crackers, several boxes of gourmet cookies and even Godiva chocolates.

"I raided everything I could think of from the gift shop," Courtney said with a warm smile.

She and Bethany poured champagne for everyone except Ella, who filled her glass with water.

"To Anna," J.D. said and she flushed as everyone lifted their glasses to her.

"And may I add," he continued, "I find it slightly ironic

that the one Wilder who chose a different path than medicine is the one who ended up saving an entire hospital."

"Hear, hear," Peter said, squeezing her arm.

The next hour would live forever in her memory. As she moved around her tiny apartment talking to first one sibling, then the next—and all three of her prospective in-laws—Anna felt eight years of loneliness begin to heal.

"You're coming to the wedding, of course," Bethany proclaimed. "I'm not taking any other answer but an enthusiastic yes."

"Of course," Anna said with a smile. "I wouldn't miss it."

It would be somewhat humiliating to show up alone when all the other Wilder siblings were conveniently paired up. Richard's image flashed in her head but she quickly shunted it aside.

She had no idea where things stood with him and her heart ached as she thought of his anger the day before.

She wanted to share the triumph of this day with him but he had made no effort to contact her. Maybe he wouldn't. After the past five days, he probably wanted nothing to do with her.

"And now on to business," Peter said suddenly, distracting her from the ache in her chest. "J.D., do you want to do the honors?"

Anna frowned, confused, as they both faced her with meaningful looks. "What business?"

"We have a proposition for you," J.D. said.

"What kind of proposition?" she asked warily.

"Obviously, Northeastern HealthCare has pulled out of talks with the hospital or we wouldn't all be here. But we still need to look to the future. It's only a matter of time before another health-care conglomerate sets its sights on the hospital. We want to head that off if we can so we're moving forward with efforts to privatize the hospital to keep it under local control."

"That won't be easy," she warned. "There are very few freestanding hospitals around anymore."

"Exactly," Peter answered. "That's why we need someone smart and savvy to be our chief financial officer and help us make this a viable enterprise. Somebody who knows the business end of things inside and out and who has ideas for making the necessary economies so we can be profitable while not sacrificing patient care."

She blinked at them, stunned at the offer. After all she had nearly done to destroy the hospital, her siblings wanted her here now to help them save it?

"You think I can do that?" she asked.

"We know you can," Peter said. "We want you to be part of this, Anna. Though I guess we should have asked first where things stand for you at NHC now."

Just a few weeks ago, she would have loved to flaunt her job offer to her siblings. Finally, she would have had proof to show her family that she could succeed in her chosen world. How could they look down on her for dropping out of medical school if she were the mergers and acquisitions vice president of a leading health-care company?

That seemed so petty now.

"I'm still considering my options," she said, content to leave it at that.

"Well, add our offer to the mix," Peter said. "We need you in Walnut River. You belong here, Anna. We can't offer you a high-powered corner office in Manhattan or the salary to match. But we can offer an opportunity to genuinely make a difference, to be part of something with the potential to make life better for everyone in this community."

She gazed at her brothers and sister as a hundred thoughts churned through her mind. They wanted her here with them. The Wilder siblings, united in a common effort to save something so important to the community and to their family. They believed in her and seemed convinced she could actually help them pull this off.

She found the idea heady and exhilarating—and terrifying.

Could she do it? She knew she could handle the challenge. Just thinking about the possibilities filled her with excitement. But how could she possibly just take the plunge straight off the steep career ladder she had been climbing at NHC the past eight years, give up all she had worked for, to stay here in Walnut River with her family to rescue one faltering hospital?

"You don't have to decide right this minute," Peter said into the silence. "It's not fair of us to spring this on you all at once. I can see you're feeling overwhelmed."

"A little," she admitted, deeply grateful they didn't expect an immediate answer.

"It's been a crazy day all the way around. Take some time to think about it. The offer will still be open tomorrow, or even after the wedding if you want to take the weekend and get back to us next week."

"I'll think about it," she promised, astonished that the idea of staying in Walnut River could hold so much appeal. Was she genuinely thinking about taking a job as

CFO for a community hospital when she could be a vice president at a major health-care industry player?

"That's all we can ask," J.D. said.

"This has been wonderful but I'm going to have to get back to the hospital," Ella said.

"Of course," Anna said. "Thank you so much for coming. It means the world to me."

"Thank you," Ella said with a hard fierce hug. "I'll call you tonight when my shift ends, okay? I have so much I want to talk to you about."

Anna smiled. "Deal. You know my ear is always here."

It was their secret code. Ear here. Tell me what's on your mind. I'm here to listen.

Ella sniffled again at Anna's words. "I'm so glad to have you back."

"Same, El."

Their sister's departure with J.D. seemed to be the signal to Peter and David and their fiancées to leave as well. In only a few moments, her apartment was quiet once more.

Anna closed the door behind David and Courtney, then slumped against it. She had forgotten how exhausting her family could be, but she wouldn't trade the last hour for anything.

She was still leaning against the door a moment later, marveling at the abrupt change in her life, when the doorbell rang. Assuming someone had left something behind, she hurried to open it then stopped dead.

Richard stood on the other side, looking wildly sexy in charcoal-gray slacks, a white dress shirt with the sleeves rolled up and a red power tie that was just a little off center.

Her heart seemed to thrum out of her chest and she

could do nothing but stare at him, her mind awash in memories of kissing him, touching him, lying in his arms.

"May I come in?" he finally asked, and she realized she must have been standing there staring at him for a full minute or more.

"I…of course," she managed and opened the door for him.

Her duplex apartment had seemed small but still comfortable with her three siblings and their prospective spouses. So why did it seem to shrink immeasurably when Richard walked inside?

She should say something. *Hello. How are you? I love you.*

The words caught in her throat and she couldn't manage to do anything but stare at him.

He was the first to break the silence.

"Why didn't you tell me?" His voice was low and intense, his eyes a heartbreaking shade of blue-green today.

"I tried," she said. Was he still angry at her? She couldn't read anything in those eyes.

"No, you didn't. Not really. You said I was misinterpreting things but you never gave me the full truth. Why didn't you tell me you knew nothing about that memo until right before I found it?"

She chewed her lip. She remembered how desperate she had been to get him out of her apartment after he had kissed her with stunning tenderness and then said such devastatingly cruel things.

"You won't like my answer."

"Try me. It can't be any worse than all the possible scenarios I've been coming up with all morning for why you didn't trust me enough to ask for my help."

She sighed. "It wasn't that. It wasn't that at all, Richard. Of course I would have trusted you if I could. But what would you have done if I'd told you the truth and enlisted your help?"

He shrugged. "I don't know. Maybe go to the media."

"You would have been on extremely shaky legal ground. As I pointed out, you had no right to access internal NHC documents. That was a confidential memo that you shouldn't have seen at all. I was afraid you would be willing to sacrifice your career by going public with what amounted to stolen information."

He stared at her, stunned. She had been trying to protect him? Of all the explanations he had considered, that one wouldn't have even made the top twenty.

"I'm the one who brought Walnut River to their attention," she continued. "I felt like I had to handle the situation on my own. To fix my own mess. If anyone's career was going to be destroyed, I wanted it to be mine, not yours. You could have been disbarred, Richard. I wasn't about to let that happen."

"Was your career destroyed?" he asked carefully.

He knew she had orchestrated the back-door coup but he had no idea where things stood for her with the new management.

She managed a smile. "I wouldn't say exactly that."

She paused. "The new chief executive officer at NHC just offered me his old job as vice president of mergers and acquisitions."

A chill swept over him and Richard thought for sure he could hear the crackle of his heart freezing solid. All the dreams he had dared let himself begin to spin turned to ice along with it.

"Vice president." He forced a laugh that sounded fake and hollow to his ears. Could she tell? he wondered. "That's amazing. Wonderful news. Congratulations."

She looked a little taken aback, as if she expected some other reaction from him. "Right. Wonderful news."

"Is that why the rest of the Wilders were here? To celebrate?" He tried to inject a little more enthusiasm in his tone. "I saw them all leaving when I pulled up. They must be so proud of you. When do you start?"

"They want me there first thing in the morning," she said, somewhat woodenly.

"What about Peter's wedding Saturday?"

"I…haven't figured that out yet."

He gripped his hand into a fist at his side, doing everything he could not to betray his pain. "Make them wait," he suggested. "If they want you badly enough, they'll have a little patience."

"Will they?" she murmured.

Did her words seem double-edged or was that simply his imagination? Richard studied her closely but her lovely features revealed nothing. He knew he was in danger of losing control in a moment so he edged closer to the door.

"Congratulations again on the job offer. I just stopped by to tell you thank you for what you did for Walnut River General. I'm sorry for jumping to the wrong conclusion before and for the things I said. I should have trusted you."

He turned to leave but she stopped him.

"Richard—"

He didn't know what she intended to say. It didn't matter. When he turned back, he thought he saw a misery in her eyes that matched the pain and loss tearing through him.

He didn't give himself time to think it through, driven only by the need to touch her one more time. He crossed the space between them in two steps and pulled her into his arms, crushing her mouth with his.

After one stunned moment, she made a tiny kind of sobbing sound and her arms slid around him, holding him as if she never wanted to let go.

He kissed her fiercely, pouring all his emotions into the embrace, doing his best to leave no doubt in her mind about how much he loved her. If she was going to leave him again, he damn well wasn't going to make it easy for her.

"Anna, don't go."

She blinked at him. "Wh-What?"

His hands were shaking, he realized with chagrin. He should just leave now before he made a bigger ass out of himself. "I shouldn't have said that. I'm sorry."

"You did, though."

"I did. I know I have no right to beg you to stay after the way I've treated you the last five days. But forget that. I'm going to beg anyway. I love you, Anna. It just about killed me when you walked away last time. I don't think I can bear losing you again. Please stay."

She stared at him, saying nothing for a long, painfully drawn-out moment, then joy flared in those beautiful blue eyes and she wrapped her arms around him again and lifted her mouth to his.

He kissed her with all the pent-up frustration and fear and longing inside him, until his insides trembled and his heart threatened to pound out of his chest.

"I love you," she said. "I love you so much. I have been absolutely miserable without you."

He framed her face with his hands, the lovely serene features he had dreamed about nearly all of his life.

"I want to marry you, Anna. I've wanted it for eight years. Longer, if you want the truth. Since we were kids studying for our calculus tests together. You are the only woman I have ever loved."

Anna closed her eyes at the sweetness of his words, at the sheer sense of rightness she found here in his arms. She had almost missed this, she thought with wonder. If she hadn't taken the assignment to return to Walnut River, she would never have found Richard again, would never have realized how very empty her life was without him.

"Yes, I'll marry you!"

"Ethan and I are a package deal. Are you sure you're okay with that?"

She thought of his darling son, with his cowlick and his mischievous smile. "Better than okay. I already love your son as much as I love you."

He kissed her again and for a long time, she forgot everything else.

"I suppose I'll have to start looking to join a firm in New York," Richard said.

She stared, shocked to her core. "But you love Walnut River."

"Not nearly as much as I love you."

The sincerity of his words humbled her. She had no idea what she had ever done to deserve a man like Richard Green but she didn't care. She was keeping him, whether she deserved him or not.

"My family has asked me to stay on and become chief financial officer for the new privately owned Walnut

River General Hospital. I'm going to call them and tell them I'm in."

He looked stunned. "Are you sure? It's a big step down from an NHC vice president."

"I'm positive," she murmured. "I want to stay right here, in Walnut River and in your arms."

He kissed her again while Lilli danced around them, and Anna knew this was one merger that was destined to succeed.

* * * * *

Mills & Boon® Special Edition
brings you a sneak preview of

Cathy Gillen Thacker's Hannah's Baby

It is the happiest day of her life when Hannah brings her adopted baby home to Texas. But what would make the new mother really happy is a daddy to complete their instant family. And Hannah's friend Joe Daugherty would make a perfect father. He just doesn't know it yet!

Don't miss this exciting new story coming next month from Mills & Boon® Special Edition, which is available in July 2009!

Hannah's Baby

by

Cathy Gillen Thacker

Hannah Callahan stood on the porch of her childhood home, savoring the cool breeze of a perfect summer morning, watching dawn streak across the vast mountains. She had grown up in Summit, Texas, and although she had spent most of her post-college years living out of a suitcase in hotels all over the world, she was glad to leave those nomad days behind her. Glad to be starting a new chapter of her life.

A dark-green Land Rover made its way up the quiet residential street.

Hannah acknowledged the driver and wrestled her suitcase down the broad wooden steps of the prairie-style home.

Thirty-five-year-old Joe Daugherty left the motor running and met her halfway up the sidewalk. He was dressed in loose fitting trousers and a vibrant striped shirt that brought out the evergreen hue of his eyes. As always, the sheer size of his rugged six-foot-three frame dwarfed her considerably smaller body.

Hannah shifted her gaze from his broad shoulders, trying not to notice how petite she felt in his presence. She and Joe had met five months earlier. He'd come into the store, and the two of them had hit it off immediately. She'd been instantly and undeniably attracted to the sexy adventurer. He had seemed similarly interested. Had she not been so ready to settle down, and had he planned to stay in the area for more than the six months it took to research and write his book, maybe they would have gotten together. But Hannah was not interested in beginning an affair that would only have to end, so they'd relegated each other to the category of casual friend, nothing more. The fact he was going on this trip with her was a fluke, the kind of favor not likely to be repeated. She needed to remember that.

The emotion simmering inside her this morning had nothing to do with the arresting features of his masculine face, or the way the short strands of his hair gleamed against the suntanned hue of his skin. Nor did it have anything to do with the amount of time she was going to be spending with Joe Daugherty over the next week. Her racing pulse was caused by the continuing tension between her and the only family she had left. Anticipation of the events to come…

Oblivious to her tumultuous thoughts, Joe slipped his strong hand beneath hers to grip the handle on her wheeled twenty-six-inch suitcase. "This all the luggage you've got?"

Hannah nodded around the sudden lump in her throat and clasped the red canvas carryall of important papers and travel necessities closer to her body. "I just need to stop by the Mercantile and say goodbye to my dad." Try one last time to talk some sense into him.

Joe fit her suitcase next to his and shut the tailgate. "No problem." He slid behind the wheel while she jumped in to ride shotgun. He looked over his shoulder as he backed out of the drive. "We've got plenty of time."

But not enough to change her dad's mind. Hannah swallowed, beset by nerves once again. "Thanks for going with me."

Joe shrugged and flashed her a sexy half smile. "Hey. It's

not every day somebody offers me an all expense paid trip to Taiwan."

"Seriously—"

"Seriously." He sent her a brief telling look that spoke volumes about his inherently understanding nature. "You need somebody to accompany you who has a current passport and no fear of the complexities of international travel. Someone who knows that particular region of Asia, not to mention the language, and is footloose and fancy-free enough to be able to drop everything and go once you got the word it was time."

Stipulations that had narrowed the field of possible travel companions considerably. Glad he was not reading anything else into the invitation she had issued him, Hannah relaxed and settled back in her seat. "Ah, the virtues of being an adventure-loving travel writer," she teased.

Joe braked for an armadillo taking his time about crossing the road. As he waited, he grinned at her. "Versus the virtues of being a marketing whiz turned entrepreneur?"

His praise made her flush. Pretending her self-consciousness had nothing to do with him, Hannah wrinkled her nose. "You can't really call me an entrepreneur since the business I'm going to run—*if* I can ever get my dad to retire—has been in the family since Summit was founded in 1847." Since then the mountain town had gone from an isolated but beautiful trading post for ranchers and settlers to a popular getaway and tourist attraction.

The armadillo finally hit the berm. Hands clasping the wheel, Joe drove on. "The changes you want to make are good ones."

He was one of the few people who had seen Hannah's plans to turn around the slowly diminishing family business. Hannah caught a whiff of cinnamon roll as they passed the bakery. "Tell that to my dad."

"I have, a time or two." Joe pressed his lips together ruefully. "Not that he's inclined to listen to an East Coast city slicker like me."

Hannah fidgeted when they stopped at a red light. She was so ready to get to Taipei and begin her new life it was ridiculous. "You grew up in Texas."

"For the first ten years of my life—" Joe waved at a prominent rancher in a pickup truck "—but I went to school in Connecticut."

While she respected Joe's Ivy League credentials, it was the inherently respectful, compassionate way he treated everyone who crossed his path that she admired. Had he intended to stay in the beautiful Trans-Pecos area of West Texas, she might have considered seeing if the two of them could be more than friends.

Unfortunately, she knew it would never happen. He was as much a vagabond at heart as she had once been. For reasons, she suspected, that were just as elusive and privately devastating as her own.

Her mother's death and her father's recent heart attack had made her face the fact that time to address old hurts—or at the very least come to terms with them—was running out. If she wanted to heal the rift between her and her dad, the way her mother had always wanted, it had to be done soon. Whether her dad cooperated or not!

Aware the silence between them had stretched on for too long, Hannah shifted her attention back to Joe and asked casually, "When will you be done with your book?" Last spring, he'd rented a cabin just outside town and used it as a home base for his research on southwest Texas.

"It's essentially done now. I just want to take one more trip to Big Bend, to check out a couple of the hotels I missed on my earlier visits, write the magazine articles I'm going to use to promote the book, and then I'm off to Australia to start my next project."

"So you'll be leaving…?"

"Texas? Right after Labor Day."

Which meant, Hannah thought sadly, she'd rarely if ever see Joe again.

In another three weeks, he'd no longer be stopping by the Mercantile to chat up the tourists shopping there about their favorite haunts in this part of Texas. He'd no longer be teasing her, or making polite conversation with her father. Or stopping by to see if she wanted to grab some lunch at one of the cafés in town, along with whomever else their age he could round up.

Joe turned onto Main Street. The county courthouse and police station sat across from the parklike grounds of the town square, taking one whole block. Farther down, brick buildings some two hundred years old sported colorful awnings over picture windows. In the past few years, restaurants that catered to tourists and natives alike had sprung up here and there, adding to the length of the wide boulevard in the center of town. But it was the imposing Callahan Mercantile & Feed that gave Summit the Old West ambience tourists loved to photograph.

Built shortly after Texas achieved statehood, the sprawling general store still bore the original log-cabin exterior. Improvements had been made over the years, but the wooden rocking chairs scattered across the covered porch that fronted the building still beckoned a person to linger, even after purchases were made.

Joe eased his SUV into a parking space in front of the store. "Any chance the day's pastries have arrived yet?"

Hannah nodded. "My dad stops by the bakery personally every morning to pick them up before he comes in. Help yourself to whatever is there. I'll go find Dad."

Gus was in back, as she figured he would be.

At seventy, he was still a handsome man with expressive brown eyes the same shade as hers. In the two years since her mother's death, his thick straight hair had turned completely white. Gus Callahan had never been an easy man. He was set in his ways. Opinionated. He had a strong sense of right and wrong and had never been known to yield to anyone. Including Hannah.

A lump formed in her throat. Wondering when she would ever stop longing for his approval, she managed to choke out, "Dad?"

He looked up from the account statements he was sorting through.

"I'm leaving," she said wishing, once again, for a miracle.

Gus scowled and set down the stack of billing notices. He looked her square in the eye and said flatly, "It's still not too late to change your mind."

From No. 1 *New York Times* bestselling author Nora Roberts

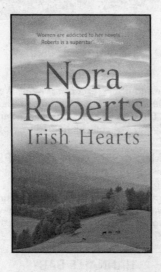

Two enthralling stories of Irish heroines with the courage to follow their dreams – and lose their hearts!

Containing the classic novels

Irish Thoroughbred

and

Irish Rose

Available 5th June 2009

0609/23a

MILLS&BOON
Special
Edition

On sale 19th June 2009

HER TEXAS LAWMAN
by Stella Bagwell

Chief Deputy Ripp McCleod didn't believe the heiress's claim that someone was stalking her. Soon it became clear that Lucita Sanchez was telling the truth and Ripp's interest in the case – and the woman – was growing very personal.

THE PRINCE'S ROYAL DILEMMA
by Brenda Harlen

Innocent Lara can't be Rowan's bride, since she wasn't born in his beautiful Mediterranean principality. The prince faces a tough choice between the country he loves and the woman who has captured his heart…

THE BABY PLAN
by Kate Little

The one thing by-the-book Julia hasn't planned on is pregnancy! Telling Sam that he's going to be a daddy might be a disaster – or it might lead to true love…

Available at WHSmith, Tesco, ASDA, and all good bookshops
www.millsandboon.co.uk

FREE!

2 Books
and a surprise gift!

We would like to take this opportunity to thank you for reading this Mills & Boon® book by offering you the chance to take TWO more specially selected titles from the Special Edition series absolutely FREE! We're also making this offer to introduce you to the benefits of the Mills & Boon® Book Club™—

- ★ **FREE home delivery**
- ★ **FREE gifts and competitions**
- ★ **FREE monthly Newsletter**
- ★ **Exclusive Mills & Boon Book Club offers**
- ★ **Books available before they're in the shops**

Accepting these FREE books and gift places you under no obligation to buy. you may cancel at any time, even after receiving your free shipment. Simply complete your details below and return the entire page to the address below. You don't even need a stamp!

YES! Please send me 2 free Special Edition books and a surprise gift. I understand that unless you hear from me, I will receive 4 superb new titles every month for just £3.19 each, postage and packing free. I am under no obligation to purchase any books and may cancel my subscription at any time. The free books and gift will be mine to keep in any case.

E9ZEF

Ms/Mrs/Miss/Mr ....Initials ....
BLOCK CAPITALS PLEASE

Surname ....

Address ....

....

....Postcode ....

Send this whole page to:
UK: FREEPOST CN81, Croydon, CR9 3WZ